CHARLESTON GRIT

A PALM COURT SUSPENSE

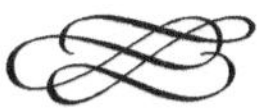

STEPHANIE EDWARDS

To Ron, my husband, for reading the roughest of drafts, helping me find the words when I get stuck, and humoring me and my wild ideas.

ISBN: 979-8-9915421-1-1

CHAPTER 1

NANCY, JULY 2010

I ain't never liked hospitals. As the scent of ammonia and bleach fills my lungs, I try not to gag. Machines beep and clank, and fluorescent lights flicker, sparking a headache. I'd rather be swallowed up by an ornery tiger shark than be here. Very few people are worth the nerves and bad memories that visiting a hospital always brings.

But there's only one Julia Caroline Mason.

My best friend stands by my side no matter what I'm goin' through. No amount of sour old mop water or the certainty that some poor soul in a nearby room is dying will make me abandon her when she needs me. Not now. Not ever.

An icy chill tingles down my spine. I hug myself to warm my arms. It's hotter than blue blazes outside, so that means one of two things: either the staff finally upgraded their ancient HVAC, or I've got an uninvited guest from the Other Side. Spirits have a way of turning the air cold, whether you see them or not. Knowing what a cheapskate the hospital administrator is, my money's on the latter. The hair on my arm stands on end. I glance around, bracing for the signature, unseen trouble only the Other Side brings.

Not a soul around. I sip the burned cafeteria coffee I bought earlier. It's terrible, but at least it's warm.

A sudden, icy burst of air sends my teeth chattering as a door flies open. My nerves jolt—I know this chill well. As I rise from the rickety waiting room chair, a young man in a hospital gown glides three feet above the floor, coming straight for me. Shoot … that confirms it: ghost trouble. Do I have a sign on my forehead that reads, "Ghost Concierge?" I pretend not to notice and slip into the nearest alcove, praying he keeps floating down the East Wing instead of following me.

I've helped my share of the deceased cross over to their Great Reward. I'm happy to help them most days, but I don't need a fixer-upper project right now. Julia Caroline is my priority. He can figure out how to go into the light without little old me.

"Hey! Can you call my wife and ask her to come and pick me up? She just left. I overheard the doctor telling the nurses they can move another patient into my room, so they must be getting ready to discharge me. I'm sure she's coming back for me, but we're running late."

Ugh. I stop in my tracks, annoyance shifting quickly into dread as I realize this spirit needs me. I'm torn between wanting to flee and feeling obligated to help.

Bless his heart—he thinks he's still alive. It's the worst when spirits can't put two and two together. Whatever common sense he had in his earthly life must have stayed behind in his decaying body. I want to run and keep ignoring him.

There's no time for this foolishness.

"Ma'am, please! It's my son's birthday. He's two today. I can't miss his party—my granny is even flying in for it. She's been so excited all week." My heart sinks. This young man is about the same age as my 24-year-old grandson, Clint. A knot forms in my throat. If Clint had a child and wife, I'd want someone to help him say goodbye to his family and cross over peacefully.

I sigh and turn around. "Hi, sugar. Listen, I've got some bad news. I'm not sure what happened—if you were sick or in an accident—but you didn't make it. I know that's hard to hear. I'll try to get a message to your wife if I can. But I need you to give me some time. I'm here with a friend for some serious tests. I can't wander too far until she's back."

The man laughs. "That is a weird thing to say. Why would you say that? No—I can't be dead. The doctor is getting ready to draw up my release papers."

Oh dear! He's in denial! I bite my lip. "What's the last thing you remember? Think real hard."

He puffs out his chest and throws up his hands. "I was just riding my motorcycle down the interstate, and something hit my back. I woke up here on the operating table about an hour ago … oh, gah!" His face falls. "I really am dead!"

I grab his hand, pat it, and sigh. "I'm so sorry, hon. That's a hard pill to swallow, to put it mildly. I'll look for your family soon. Please go rest and meet me here in an hour."

"Thank you, ma'am." He nods and fades into a silvery mist.

Thank goodness! Relief washes over me as I let out a sigh. If I'm lucky, he's found his way home—either his residence down here or his final destination—it doesn't make a bit of a difference to me.

Before I return to the waiting room, I stop by the soda vending machines. They're sold out except for diet cola. I gag. No thanks. I'd rather guzzle gasoline topped with slimy gator guts.

What I wouldn't give for a pitcher of sweet tea right now! I imagine sipping one on my porch swing with Julia Caroline—her infectious laugh filling the air. For a moment, a rush of longing replaces my unease, brightening my mood as I recall the joy she brings, even now.

I've wet my pants while giggling with her more times than I can count on all my fingers and toes. It even happened to us when we were young, before our bladders gave up the ghost.

What if the doctor's doom and gloom prognosis is right? This can't be our last summer of front porch sitting.

We're not old yet. I glance at my wrinkled hands. Okay, maybe we are, but we're not ancient.

"Ahem—most people read palms from the other side of their hands. Are you finding anything interesting?" I look up to see Julia Caroline covering a wicked grin while standing by a vending machine. *How is she so cheerful? Maybe she got some good news. Please, Lord!*

"That was so quick! Did they tell you anything?" My heart palpitates. I try to think of something uplifting to calm my nerves, but nothing comes to mind.

She shakes her head. "You know how these darn things go. It's always a waiting game when it comes to getting results from any doctor. But I'm not worried. It's in the Lord's hands. Everything's going to come back negative, and we'll take another one of our wild and crazy road trips down the coast. Our kids will worry about us the whole time, but we'll have the best vacation of our lives." Her eyes sparkle.

Wouldn't that be wonderful? Reality intrudes. She needs to face facts—the odds are against her.

I start to argue, but I stop myself. If Julia Caroline believes this lovely fairytale, who am I to discourage her? I've read about the power of positive thinking for cancer patients. I can only hope her optimism will save her.

Tears tug at the corners of my eyes, but I force a smile. "Let's go the long way home through Sullivan's Island and stop at Acme Cantina for some shrimp and a couple of cocktails?"

"Well, it isn't an all-inclusive trip to the Bahamas, but it's a good start." She winks at me. "I'll never turn down lunch at Acme. If I do, you should be worried."

I giggle, but the joy is pierced by a nagging sensation in the pit of my stomach. Worry returns, shadowing the laughter. What if she's wrong about her health? We've never lived more than a few blocks apart. She is my sister in every way but by blood relation. I've never paid heed to that, though. When it comes to us, blood isn't thicker than water. The water might be salty sometimes, but it's the water that counts.

Rubbing my temples, I close my eyes and try to push negative thoughts out of my mind. If she is staying optimistic, I need to support her decision. Freaking out won't help anyone.

She frowns and puts her arm around my shoulder. "Are you okay? I know how much you hate hospitals. Let's get outta here." I nod but remember my promise to the young man. I groan. More than anything, I want to leave and enjoy a heaping plate of creek shrimp and a margarita on the rocks at Acme. But I can't go back on my word.

"Ugh. I need to do one more thing before we go home. You can start the car and crank the AC. I'm sure it's hot enough to boil a whole pot of grits on the dashboard today."

Sighing, I toss my keys to her. Reluctance weighs heavy in my chest—duty overrides resistance as I resolve to follow through. It's the right thing to do.

I wander back to the hallway where I last saw him, but no one is around. I pick up a magazine from an adjacent table to busy my hands. Several nurses pass me in a hurry, making a beeline for the front door. It must be time for a shift change. Who can blame these gals for running out the door at quitting time?

I try not to make eye contact with anyone. With ghosts, meeting a gaze means risking being chosen as their designated escort to the Other Side. *No thanks!* After pacing for about fifteen minutes, I give up. I can't keep Julia Caroline waiting. A knot forms in my stomach. I hate leaving the man hanging. But what if he's crossed over? I don't know his name or how to find his family. I did my best to help. I whisper a prayer that he found his way to Heaven.

Walking out to the car, I wipe my sweaty palms on my linen slacks. *Ick!* I've got to shake off this unsettled feeling so I can enjoy the afternoon with my best friend.

Where did I park? This is always a problem for my scattered brain!

Rockabilly music blares from a car radio and grabs my attention. In the distance, Julia Caroline is sitting in my car, flourishing her arms and nodding her head in time to the music. I have to laugh. *Never a dull moment with this nut!* At least she isn't hard to track down in a crowded parking lot.

I open the car door, and she leans toward the driver's seat and croons, "Oh, baby!"

"You're a mess." I smile. "I guess you could say the same about me. If we have to get older, at least we're gonna be two silly old biddies together. Nothin' better."

"Nothin' at all. We got to raise our babies, but now that they're grown, they have their own lives. And there ain't a single eligible bachelor I'm interested in being charmed by. Dating ain't worth the drama. Besides, I gave my heart away to James a long time ago. At the end of the day, you're the one I want to be with. We have the most fun when we're together."

This is exactly why she can't leave me behind! No one else makes me laugh or smile the way this woman does. Other than my boys, she is the greatest blessing the good Lord has given me.

CHAPTER 2

When we park at Acme, four police cruisers zoom past, sirens wailing and lights flashing.

My heart races as I look over at Julia Caroline. Without a word, we jump out of the car and run across the street to the police department. Another half a dozen patrol cars race by, and I scan the parking lot for Clint's cruiser. I can't stand worrying about my boy every time there is an emergency. I despised it when his father, my son Wesley, was on patrol, too.

Julia Caroline places her hand on my shoulder. "Don't worry yet. He's probably helping someone who needs him. Just breathe. We'll ask someone what's going on."

I nod and draw in a few rapid breaths. But it's no use, my heart isn't in my chest. It's in the line of duty, doing Heaven only knows what. *Please, Lord, watch over my sweet babe.* Thank goodness Clint's brothers had the good sense to go into less risky professions like accounting, teaching, and podiatry. I couldn't bear the worry of having more than one first responder in the family.

The police station door has never felt so heavy. I push the metal bar with all my might and gasp when I enter the lobby.

Phones are ringing, and the scratchy static of police scanners fills the room.

Where is the receptionist? Connie is usually right here, asking to see pictures of Clint's nieces and nephews and helping me tease Clint about finding a nice girl to settle down with. As much as I love chatting about my family, I'm relieved I don't need to entertain any small talk this morning. I just need to be sure Clint is safe.

An officer I haven't seen before bursts through the back door and looks over at us. "I'll be with y'all in just a minute."

He proceeds to answer several phone calls and types something on the computer sitting on Connie's desk. What on earth is taking so long? I'm trying to be patient, but a grandmother can only handle so much.

Julia Caroline pulls me aside and squeezes my hand. "Cut it out, Nan. You're boring holes in that poor man's head, and your crossed arms speak volumes about your attitude. Try to stay calm. Something big is brewing, and that's his priority. He'll help you as soon as he can."

I shoot her a dirty look and resist the urge to stick out my tongue. "You're telling me you'd be calm if your girls were in danger?"

She smirks. "No, of course not. But you'd be telling me to cool it right now. I'm returning the favor in advance. I'm sure I'll need to cash it in, eventually."

I put my head in my hands. "I'm sure you're right." She always is. "Alright, Miss Smarty Pants, let's sit down until this nice officer can talk to us."

My nerves are jumping around like a Palmetto bug trapped inside a Mason jar. I'll probably cry if I try to say anything to Julia Caroline. So, I pretend to lose myself in my social media feed as I mindlessly scroll my phone. In reality, I don't give two hoots about reading about Lorraine Baxter's new-to-her RV or the shenanigans Shirley McAbee's feral hound dog has caused today. Our neighborhood would be better off if both offenders were taken to the junkyard.

"Ma'am, sorry for your wait. How can I help you?"

Julia Caroline snaps her fingers near my face. "Hey! Earth-to-Nancy! The officer is ready to talk to you."

I snap out of my scrolling coma … a trap I swore I'd never fall into. Here I am, though—I'm just as bad as all these young people with their heads stuck in their phones. I jump up from my chair and walk up to the reception area. How do I even ask the questions rolling through my mind? I smack the top of my head as the officer stares at me.

"Are you okay, ma'am? Is there something I can do to help?"

I nod. "I'm Clint Parsons' grandmother. A bunch of patrol cars just flew down Palm Boulevard. Clint's car isn't here. Could you tell me if he's okay?"

"Let me check." He looks down at the computer in front of him, clicks several keys and stares at the screen for what seems like eternity. His silence doesn't sit well with me. *Why isn't he saying something? For land's sake—how long is it going to take to find out if my baby is safe?*

He sighs. Oh, no! He's going to tell me something awful. I just know it in my bones. This is one of the plumb worst days of my life. First, Clint's mama and daddy, my Wesley, left this world much too young. Clint can't do the same.

My arm shakes, and sweat pours down my face.

Please, Lord, give me strength not to pass out in the police station. The shaking suddenly calms, and I realize Julia Caroline is holding me upright. She is my rock in every sense of the word. I can't lose her and Clint at the same time. Clint's brothers are my other loves, but they all scattered after graduating high school and have built lives elsewhere. I don't blame them. Not everyone can find their calling so close to home. Poor Clint. He's just gotta be safe!

I try to fake a smile, but I'm sure I look insane. "Officer, I just want to find out if he's okay. I know you can't give me details about what he is doing or where he is."

"Ma'am, your grandson isn't accounted for right now. It's probably just a glitch in our system, but I can't find him. I'm sorry I can't provide a definitive answer. I can take your number and call you after we locate him."

I gasp. "How do you lose an officer? Can't you radio him or call his phone? What about his new partner, Mario Rodriguez—Connie's son? She was so excited that he moved here from California last week. Why can't you reach him?"

He looks down at his hands. "I tried Clint's phone, and he didn't answer. I would love to tell you more right now, but I can't. What is your cell phone number? I'll call you or ask Clint to reach out as soon as possible."

This doesn't sound good. He definitely knows more than he's sharing.

I grip the reception desk with white knuckles and lock eyes with the officer. "Look, I understand you can't give me the details. I just want to know if my grandson is alive. I don't care about anything else. Can't you help with that at least?"

He shakes his head and points at the computer. "I'm sorry. I can't make the darn contraption do something it doesn't want to. I'll touch base with everyone who works with Clint to see what I can find out. In the meantime, go eat some dinner, and go home to rest. You're worrying yourself when we don't have the facts."

My nostrils flare, and I place my hands on my hips. "Do you have any children?" He nods. "Two boys and one girl."

"Wouldn't you do the same thing if you thought one of them was in danger?"

He hangs his head down low and sighs. "You're right. I would definitely be tracking them down, no matter the consequences. Trust me, though; our officers' safety is a priority here. I've sent a group text to the whole PD to find out about Clint. I'm sure I'll hear back soon. Go to Acme and eat some dinner. If

I haven't called by the time you're done eating, come back over, and we'll figure something out."

I nod and thank him even though I'm still not satisfied. I don't want to be thrown in jail for harassing an officer. Besides, it's not going to help me find Clint.

After we walk outside, Julia Caroline rubs my shoulder. "I'm sure he's fine, Nan. Let's do what the nice officer suggested. You'll feel better after you have some food in your stomach."

"I hear you, but my heart doesn't. It doesn't listen to reason … not when it comes to my babies. I need to know he is okay, and then I'll be fine. I wish Clint had found a less dangerous career, but this was his calling. His dad's, too. If Clint has children, I hope they stay far away from law enforcement work. I'll be so old by then; my ticker won't be able to handle it. I'm barely holdin' up now."

As we walk into Acme, the weathered screen door clanks behind us. The dimly lit restaurant comforts me like an old friend. These wood-paneled walls have seen many of our family celebrations and sad occasions. It's our retreat when things go wrong and our place to celebrate. Acme is an extension of our home.

Sabrina, the manager, runs over to welcome us and takes us to our usual booth in the back corner. She doesn't bother bringing us menus before running to the kitchen to place our order, and I laugh to myself—we're that predictable.

Julia Caroline raises an eyebrow. "Was that a smile on your face? You doing okay?"

I roll my eyes. "I'm worried … terrified, but I was just thinking we should shake things up and try something different from the menu sometime, so people won't think we're boring."

She smirks. "Why would we do something silly like that? We know what we want, and there ain't nothin' wrong with ordering what we enjoy. If people have a problem with it, well … they can kiss my extra salty grits."

I giggle. Julia Caroline's brand of sass is my favorite. The tightness in my chest eases a bit. She's trying to lighten my mood, and I love her for it.

Julia Caroline stands up from the table. "Food always comes to the table when someone goes to the bathroom. So, I'm gonna powder my nose. I'm so hungry I could eat five pounds of shrimp on my own. Be right back."

The television in the corner flickers and catches my attention. A picture of a familiar young man flashes up on the screen. I wince—where do I recognize him from? He appears to be about the same age as Clint. Oh, my goodness—it's the man from the hospital! I clutch my pearls and try not to scream.

CHAPTER 3

$\mathcal{I}$ stand and move closer, so I can hear what the news reporter is saying.

"Isle of Palms Police Department Officer Mario Rodriguez was shot today while driving his motorcycle down I-26 near North Charleston. No suspects are being held at this time. Officer Rodriguez was off duty and headed to a doctor's appointment at the time of the incident. His mother, Connie Rodriguez, also works at the police department. We have Police Chief Gerald Baker here to give more details."

My stomach lurches, and I freeze in place. *That clean-shaven, bald man was Mario?* I hadn't seen the boy since he graduated from high school. Back then, he wore glasses, tie-dye T-shirts, baggy jeans, a long ponytail, and a goatee.

This can't be real. What are the odds that his unfortunate soul found me at the hospital?

That's why Connie wasn't at the police department. My heart sinks—poor Connie! If Mario was off duty when the shooting happened, where is Clint? Is he even working today? If not, why isn't he answering my calls or texts? My hands are shaking. I clasp them together to try to calm them, but no luck.

"Nan, you okay? You look like you've seen a ghost. Oh dear, have you?" I turn to see Julia Caroline staring at me. "Come sit down and tell me what's going on."

"No. We gotta find Clint. I'll tell you on the way back to the police department."

Julia Caroline pays for our food, which Sabrina has already packaged into to-go containers.

Sabrina wipes the corners of her eyes with a handkerchief. "When I heard about Mario, I figured you'd need to hit the road. It's such a tragedy. He came in with Clint for lunch every day last week. He was so psyched about his kid's birthday party. I feel awful for Connie, too."

I hug the sweet young woman. I keep hoping Clint will take a shine to her, if he can ever move on from being in love with Julia Caroline's granddaughter, Blake. I understand why he fell hard for Blake. I love her like one of my own, myself. Those two were a match made in heaven from birth, but young love often goes awry. It's been six years since they broke up. Clint deserves to find someone else.

As we leave Acme and walk toward the police department, I fill Julia Caroline in on everything I heard on the news and my conversation with Mario at the hospital. My stomach churns with every step.

"Oh, goodness, no! Not Connie's boy! She'd just convinced him to move here with his wife and baby ... no wonder you were acting wacky earlier."

"I feel horrible for not helping him, but I couldn't find him when I went back."

Julia Caroline waves her hands. "There's nothing you could have done differently. Don't beat yourself up. Let's go find Clint."

Before I open the door to the police station, I draw a ragged breath. *Please, God, let my boy be alright.* Best case scenario, he's distraught over losing his partner and friend. Of course, he's not okay. But if he's safe, we'll work through all the rest together.

He can take a leave of absence and relax for a couple of weeks. That might be the ticket for him. He works too hard.

The door jingles as we enter the lobby. *Has it always done that?* If so, I haven't noticed. My nerves must be extra raw.

I walk up to the reception desk, and the officer looks up. "I was just about to call you. Clint is fine. Today is his day off. He was out fishing in Murrell's Inlet this morning and got home about an hour ago. That's why we haven't been able to reach him all day."

Tears fill my eyes, and I muster to mouth, "Thank you."

Julia Caroline puts her arm around me and kisses my cheek. "I'm so relieved, too, Nan! Let me talk to the officer for a bit. Go sit down, and I'll be right there."

I plop down on the hard wooden bench and try to collect my bearings. Digging through my purse, I find a pack of tissues, my compact, and a tin of mints. Checking out my red puffy eyes, I gasp—Clint can't see me like this. I wipe my eyes and dab on a bit of powdered foundation to hide my splotchy, tear-stained appearance. And I pop a mint into my mouth, hoping it will calm my nerves.

A few moments later, Julia Caroline offers her hand to help me up from the bench, and I laugh. "I'm not that feeble yet."

"No, but you've had a doozy of a day. C'mon silly. Let's go see your boy."

As we walk back to the car, I ask a question I'm almost certain I don't want answered. "You were over there for a while. What did you say to the officer?"

Julia Caroline frowns. "I asked if Clint knows about Mario yet. I wanted you to be prepared before we head over to his house."

I gulp. I shoulda kept my mouth shut. "What did he say?" The tears rolling down her cheeks told me everything I needed to know. *Heavens—how am I going to tell my boy his partner is gone?* He's so young and dedicated to his job. And Mario had already become more than a coworker. Clint needed a best friend.

Connie needed her son. And I haven't met them, but I'm positive Mario's wife and baby needed him, too.

We're not supposed to question things, but why do some people die young? They have so much left to accomplish in life. It hardly seems right.

The drive from Acme to Clint's house is a blur. I run through every possible way to break the news to my grandson. I love his tender heart most days. It makes him kind, empathetic and a good cop, but today, it's going to shatter into a million pieces.

No amount of hugs or homemade peach cobbler will help Clint feel better, but that doesn't mean I won't try. It's my job as his grandmother.

When Julia Caroline parks her car in Clint's driveway, I run across the shell and sand path to the front door and knock a little too hard. *Calm down; acting like a fool isn't the ticket.* I draw a deep breath and stand back.

The door opens, and Clint is wearing his goofy fishing hat, baggy camo cargo shorts and a tank top, with zinc oxide smeared on his nose. I try to hold back a laugh, but my nerves are at an all-time high. Once one chuckle escapes my mouth, I can't control the others that follow. Unfortunately, this is how my brain deals with extreme stress sometimes. I'm not proud of how my mind reacts, but I can't help it.

Julia Caroline walks up beside me and shakes my arm. "What's the matter with you? Do you think this is really the time to be laughing like a drunk hyena?"

It's inappropriate, but I can't stop myself from laughing and pointing at Clint. Somehow, I manage to squeak out, "He just looks so ridiculous."

Clint scratches his head. "Hey, now. I didn't ask you to come here and make fun of me. I'm just trying to protect my skin, so I don't look like an old wrinkly man before I'm even forty years old. What's wrong with that?"

Julia Caroline sighs. "Nothin.' Her nerves are just rattled, making her act loony. You know how she gets." She glares at me over the top of her reading glasses. "I'm afraid we have some bad news to share with you. Let's go sit down. I'm sure she'll get over her giggle fest in a minute."

We walk through the small entryway to Clint's living room and sit down on the sofa while he runs to the kitchen.

He brings us three sodas and plops down on his oversized armchair. "Okay. You have my full attention. What is so important? You've got me worried."

I hold my chest and squinch my eyes together. I haven't shared such horrible news with Clint since his parents died in a car accident when he was in kindergarten. He is the oldest of five boys and the only one who truly remembers their parents. The night my Wesley and his lovely MaryAnne died remains the worst day of my life. This might be a close second.

Clint's face falls as I break the news to him, and my stomach turns upside down. For a moment, he resembles the scared little boy from that horrible night.

I get up to console him. "I'm so sorry, Sugar. It's unimaginable that something like this could happen to Mario. I know you'd gotten close again. I wish I could do something to help you feel better."

All the color drains from Clint's face. *Oh, no—is he going to pass out?*

"You look right peaked. Do you need some water? Have you eaten today? I can make you a sandwich or something quick."

He waves his hand. "I'm okay … err … I don't know what I am, but I don't need anything. I was just thinking about the last thing Lauren, Mario's wife, told me when I picked up the phone at the station yesterday. She was gonna tell him she is pregnant at their son's birthday party today. She asked me to pick up a special cake from the bakery for him. I was getting ready to pick it up and head over to their house." He gestures toward an awkwardly wrapped gift, clearly a toy truck for Mario's son.

I never ask if things could get worse because they always can. But good gravy, this is the absolute pits!

Clint sighs. "I don't know what to do. I'm sure Lauren and Connie are a wreck. I want to help somehow. Would y'all mind going with me? You're both better with the touchy-feely woman stuff than I am."

I nod. "Of course. We'll go with you, but are you sure you're okay? It's alright to take some time for yourself. He was your partner and your friend."

"No. I need to go see them. It's the right thing to do."

He always puts others first. I'm so proud to be his grandmother.

CHAPTER 4

We pile into Clint's Jeep, and he drives to Mario and Lauren's house. As we cross the Ravenel Bridge, I stare at the floorboard so no spirits can make eye contact with me.

With paranormal activity, bridges are bad juju on a good day. On a bad day, well, I can't even go there right now. Let's just say, with my nerves being shot, I don't need hitchhiking spirits to join us. I'm not great at pretending I don't see someone or saying "no," especially after unknowingly blowing off Mario this morning.

Better safe than sorry.

Clint takes the second downtown exit. We meander down the oak-lined side streets past businesses and colorfully painted homes until we reach the quiet Radcliffe community near the College of Charleston. Although I have lived in the Lowcountry my entire life, I haven't spent much time in this area.

A chill tingles down my spine as he pulls up to a brick house with shutters painted Charleston green—a shade so dark it's nearly black.

What's so unsettling about a beautifully restored home with

a manicured lawn? The people inside are hurting over losing Mario, and I'm heartbroken for them all. But that's not what's itching me.

I can't put my finger on the problem, but trouble always has a way of revealing itself. *Ugh. That's for sure.*

Clint parks in front of the house, and I try to shake off my uneasiness as I undo my seatbelt and jump down from the Jeep's running board. I walk up onto the wraparound porch and close my eyes. How am I going to help this family? I've lost both a husband and a child. No one should have to bury someone so young.

Someone squeezes my hand. I don't have to open my eyes to know it's Julia Caroline, but I'll look like an idiot if my eyes are closed when Lauren opens the door. I look over at my best friend, and she's staring at me.

She winces. "You thinking about Wesley?"

I give a slight nod, not wanting to get into an emotional conversation. It wouldn't be right to dump my baggage on Lauren when she's already dealing with so much.

Clint rings the doorbell, and I look away. *This is going to be hard.*

A young woman with bouncy blonde curls opens the door. Her bloodshot eyes and the hollerin' toddler behind her tell me everything I need to know. This lady hasn't slept well since her baby was born. Now, she is facing the reality of raising this young'un and the baby who's on the way by herself.

Clint introduces us to Lauren and little Georgie, who is still wailing.

Julia Caroline takes Lauren's hand. "Is it okay if I tend to Georgie?"

Lauren nods while rubbing her eyes. "Thank you. He needs a nap and a snack. There's some fruit and juice in the fridge." She gestures toward the kitchen, and Julia Caroline runs in that direction.

I try not to stare at Lauren's shaky hands. "Hon, why don't

you come sit down with me on the sofa? Julia Caroline has raised many babies, both hers and mine. Little Georgie is in great hands. Do you need me to call anyone for you? Your mama or a friend? You shouldn't be alone now."

Lauren shakes her head and wipes her nose with a tissue. "All my family and friends live in California. I haven't found a job or made friends yet. My dad is coming here in a couple of days, but no one can come today."

"What about Connie? She was so excited when y'all decided to move here and couldn't wait to have her family around."

"No. It wouldn't be right to ask her to help now. She's struggling herself. I don't want to bother her."

"I bet she would love to be with you and Georgie, and she's only a short drive away."

Lauren bursts into tears and buries her face in a handkerchief. I pat the young woman's back and try to console her. I can't imagine what she's going through right now. My abusive ex-husband cheated on me, and I kicked him to the curb when Wesley was little. Brian, the only man I've ever truly cared about, moved away a few months into our blossoming romance to care for his dying daughter.

After she passed, he stayed to help raise her children. I knew he wouldn't come home. As predicted, we lost touch after a while, and a few years ago, his cousin told me he was getting married. By then, I'd moved on too … determined to be an old maid.

My thoughts turn to Wesley. If his wife, MaryAnne, had survived their wreck, I would have supported her, no matter how badly I was hurting.

Doesn't Connie deserve the same chance?

Lauren sits upright, and I try to smile. "Look, honey, I really think Connie should come to stay with you. Would you like Clint to pick her up, or do you want to go back to the island with us? I'm sure she is going to want to be with y'all. She loves you both."

She dries her eyes and takes a sip of water from an oversized cup. "Okay. I'll call her."

I pat her shoulder and hop up. "I'll give you some privacy. I'm gonna check on Julia Caroline and Georgie."

The baby's coos filter through the screen door to the sunroom. When I step outside, Clint is driving toy trucks in circles around Georgie. My heart swells at the sight. He will make an incredible dad someday.

While playing, the child drops his truck, claps, and squeals, "Yay, Daddy!" Oh, goodness—he's confused. I remember both Wesley and his boys being that age. Every man is "Daddy," and every woman is "Mama."

Clint pats Georgie on the head. "Hey, cutie. I'm not your daddy. He was a great man and really loved you."

Georgie stomps his feet. "No—Daddy!"

"That's right. I'm Uncle Clint, not your daddy."

Georgie runs past Clint and waves furiously at a seemingly empty corner. "Daddy! My dada! I lubb you, Daddy!"

Julia Caroline grabs my hand, but I keep my eyes locked on Georgie. He believes he is talking to someone. Is Mario really there?

I don't see anyone, and I can't call out to him with everyone around. That would be hard to explain to Lauren, and Clint would be beside himself with embarrassment. My sixth sense doesn't sit well with him. He's been clear about that anytime I've tried to talk about my paranormal experiences.

Clint squints and shrugs. "I don't see anything. Kids sure have active imaginations."

I lock eyes with Julia Caroline. This ain't our first supernatural rodeo. In our collection of bizarre and wild otherworldly experiences, when someone thinks they're seeing or hearing a dead person, they usually are.

Little ones are more open to the idea of ghosts being real until they reach the age where they stop playing make believe. To make matters worse for Georgie, he is so young that he wouldn't grasp the concept of Mario's death. To him, his daddy being there is normal.

Lauren pokes her head into the room and massages her temples. "Connie asked us to come stay with her for a few days. It's hard to leave our place, even though we haven't been here for long. But I don't know the first thing about planning a funeral or how to ..." She sighs and holds her chest. "Do this parenting thing on my own. Mario was the best dad and husband. He didn't even know about the baby yet." She wipes a tear from her cheek.

Clint hugs her. "I'm so sorry. I loved working with Mario. We had a lot of fun growing up together on the island. Miss Connie was sure excited to have him come back home with you and Georgie. It's all she talked about for the entire month before you got here. She's a nice lady." He leans down to Georgie and smiles. "And she makes the best chocolate chip cookies I've ever eaten. You're lucky to have her as your grandma."

Georgie's eyes sparkle. "Lubb, Grandma! Cookie, cookie!"

My heart leaps on Connie's behalf, and I hug the little guy.

"Your grandma is going to need to hear you say that a whole bunch. Tell her as much as you can."

Georgie toddles off singing, mostly gibberish with an occasional "Grandma" or "cookie" thrown into the song.

Julia Caroline and I help Lauren pack up clothing, diapers, toys ... everything a mom and toddler might need for a few days away from home. After we finish, Clint offers to carry everything out and move Georgie's car seat from Lauren's car to his Jeep.

Lauren takes Georgie outside to buckle him up and says she'll be right back to lock up. The cutie waves at me through the front window. *What a sweetheart!*

Julia Caroline nudges me. "Now's our chance."

I nod. "Mario—if you're here, we want to help. We have to go. We're taking your family to your mom's house on Isle of

Palms. Julia Caroline and I'll be watching for you. Please come see us when you can."

He doesn't materialize, and I scratch my head. "What do you think is going on here? Do you think he's still around?"

Julia Caroline frowns. "Sometimes a newly deceased spirit doesn't understand how to appear, or they go into what's almost like a hibernation mode. With Georgie seeing him, I don't think he's gone for good yet. My hunch is he's sticking around for his family."

Please, Lord, if this young man's spirit is still unsettled and hasn't left for his Heavenly home, send him to us, so we can help him find peace.

I don't feel right leaving without talking to Mario, but we need to get Lauren and Georgie settled at Connie's house.

CHAPTER 5

On the way to the island, I worry that we have abandoned Mario. A gnawing sensation eats away at my stomach. Hopefully, he will figure out how to reach us. Most ghosts can easily travel among places where they've formed memories.

If Mario made it from the hospital to his house, he should be able to figure out how to reach Isle of Palms.

I should study up on this sort of thing, since I often get sucked into helping ghosts during their transition to their final resting place. Fortunately, most spirits I meet just want me to share a message with their family before they cross over.

During the short trip to the island, Georgie's precious babble comforts me. I miss my grandkids being this little and can't wait for the next generation of babies to be born. Three of Clint's brothers married young, so I'm guessing it won't be too much longer before someone makes me a great-grandmother. Children are truly Heaven's most special blessings. I've loved every minute with all mine.

Julia Caroline can't take her eyes off Georgie's cherub-like, dimpled face either.

When she locks her gaze with mine, I know what's on her mind—we'd both wished for Clint and Blake to put aside their differences and realize they should be together. Those two would make some beautiful babies.

I ain't giving up until one of them gets hitched to someone else. Years ago, I would have said, "I hope that day never comes." But no one deserves to be lonely, least of all, them. I love them so much my heart might pop. I'll proudly attend both their weddings, even though I might secretly wish the bride and groom were different people.

As we reach the Isle of Palms Connector, the salty air tickles my nose, and the rising tide in the marsh flats sets my soul at ease. *Home, sweet home! Ain't nothing like it!*

Families loaded down with beach chairs, backpacks, and coolers flood the streets—typical summer crowd. I can't blame them. Our island is pretty magical, from the sparkling Atlantic Ocean to the mysterious Spanish moss that drapes down our ancient oak trees and whips in the wind even on the calmest of days.

I can't help but envy the people whose biggest concern today is avoiding a sunburn. *Lucky them.*

After passing the front beach area, the pedestrian traffic thins out. My shoulders relax, and I close my eyes. We islanders are grateful for the money tourism brings to our small community, but at the same time, the unrelenting crowds can drain our energy when we're seeking peace.

When I open my eyes, Clint turns into Connie's neighborhood. A line of mighty oaks divides the boulevard and provides a cooling canopy, a welcome respite from the sun's blazing rays.

Connie's adorable white cottage with a turquoise door and gray hurricane shutters oozes with island charm.

It's hard to believe Mario left this house for college six years ago. I remember the day clearly. Clint helped him load boxes to be shipped to Los Angeles into the mail truck.

Connie waited until Mario had left for the airport before

breaking down in tears. Her only son was leaving her alone in a vast house. I reassured her he would return someday. I thought he would be around a lot longer than a couple of weeks. My heart aches for her. Life has a way of kicking you when you think something good might happen for once.

Losing Wesley about broke me, but having his children around kept my heart and life full. Hopefully, having Lauren and Georgie here will help Connie in the same way.

As Clint parks the Jeep, Lauren breaks into tears. I get out of the vehicle and open her door.

"Oh, hon. Golly, you're going through the wringer. Let me help you." I give her my hand as she steps down onto Connie's driveway. "I know it doesn't seem like it right now, but things will get better. Life is so dang unfair. Why don't you go inside? We'll bring Georgie and all your things."

Lauren takes a tissue out of a skirt pocket and dabs at the tears pooling on her cheeks before stepping up on the porch and ringing the doorbell. The door opens, and I hear Connie's twangy voice as Lauren walks into the house.

Georgie snores, tugging on my heartstrings. *What a cutie pie!* He's so content—I'd love nothing more than to let him sleep. I wipe a bead of sweat from his face. It's too hot to sit out here. I hate it, but we're going to have to wake him.

I let out a deep exhale. *What a day!*

Julia Caroline wipes her brow. "It's hotter than blue blazes! Even Satan's sweatin' today. Let's take this lil' one inside before we all melt." She unclips the car seat harness and pulls him close to her body.

"You've still got the magic touch, Granny Mason." I wink.

"Once a granny, always a granny. I can't wait for our grands to have their babies. It's going to be divine."

"Won't it be? I'm sure it will do Connie's heart some good to hug this little dumplin'."

We let ourselves inside, and somehow, Georgie stays asleep. *Thank God for little miracles.*

As we make our way through the foyer, the sunlight from an arched window bathes us in a golden glow. Persian rugs in rich jewel tones accent the hallway leading to the living room. Connie's home always offers a warm, inviting respite from life. I've only been inside a handful of times, despite having been friends for decades.

She usually comes to my place … a habit we started when I had five young'uns living under my roof, and she had just Mario to raise. It made more sense to bring her one quiet, calm child to my chaotic house full of silly monkeys.

Connie's voice echoes from back in the hall, so I lead the way, allowing Julia Caroline to follow behind while holding Georgie tight to her chest.

When we reach the kitchen, we find Connie and Lauren nursing highball glasses of sweet tea. The Atlantic sparkles just twenty yards away from the sliding glass door to the deck. On any other day, the beauty of the setting would have overwhelmed me. But today ain't that day; it's one of sadness and grief.

Georgie's eyes light up when he sees his grandmother. He tears away from Julia Caroline's arms and runs to Connie, who promptly picks him up and kisses his forehead.

"Grandma! I lubb you berry much!"

Connie draws a deep, ragged breath. "I love you, baby." She wipes a tear from her cheek, pulls Georgie closer, and rests her chin on his head.

I place my hand on Connie's arm. "Hon, we'll do anything for y'all. We're gonna give you some time to heal without needing to play hostess. We'll be back with dinner tonight. If you need us to take Georgie at any point, just holler. We've become as thick as thieves already."

Connie whispers her thanks, which is hushed by Georgie's outburst. "Daddy! Hey, where you go, Daddy? Dadda?"

Clint kneels and locks eyes with Georgie. "Buddy, your

daddy had to go away. He went to Heaven to be with Jesus. But he loved you, your mama, and grandma very much."

God love Clint—he's so steady and calm in challenging situations, which is one reason he's a great police officer.

Georgie shakes his head. "No! My Daddy is right there. He's waving at me." He points to the kitchen doorway, leading into the hallway. A silvery shadow flickers around the door frame. I squint. Is that Mario? We can't call for him without knowing if Connie believes that spirits linger after death or can visit from the Other Side. *Does she see and hear him, too?*

My gaze meets Connie's. She doesn't say anything right away. It's not my place to confirm what he's seeing or to possibly contradict his family's beliefs.

When she starts to comfort Georgie, her lip quivers. "Baby, Clint is right. It's so unfair that you had to lose your daddy … that we all did. But he sure loved you to pieces." She closes her eyes and sucks in a series of deep breaths.

Where is Julia Caroline? I didn't see her leave the kitchen. I excuse myself and return to the living room, but she isn't there, and she isn't in the powder room. She didn't vanish into thin air, so what in the heck is she doing? Footsteps outside catch my attention, and I peek out the window. She's talking to seemingly no one. *Aha!*

I join her outside, but I still don't see anyone else. "Who were you talking to?"

She winces. "Mario. He hasn't crossed over yet, but he disappeared right as you walked outside."

"Why can't we see and hear him when Georgie can?"

Julia Caroline shifts her weight to the other foot. "From what Mario said, it sounds like there is a malevolent spirit following him around and holding him back in the Great In-Between. Sometimes, when aggressive people die and don't cross over immediately, they turn into pure evil spirits. We've gotta help Mario go to his final resting place for his sake and his family's. If Georgie keeps seeing him, it's going to be confusing and frustrating for all of them. And it could be dangerous if the other ghost gains more power."

"So being a jerk makes someone stronger in death than a person who was kind when they were alive?"

"Yeah. They can be more powerful and incredibly dangerous to everyone they encounter, especially the nice guys like Mario."

I stomp my foot. *Why does the paranormal world have to be so dang complex and unfair?* If anyone can solve this mystery, it's Julia Caroline. She ain't afraid of nothin' or no one, dead or alive.

CHAPTER 6

After we check on Connie and her family again, we excuse ourselves to give them some space.

When we get into the Jeep, Clint grips the steering wheel so tightly his knuckles turn white. On the outside, he appears to take everything in stride, but he is more sensitive than he lets on to others. How can I help him?

I rest my hand on his shoulder. "Are you holding up okay?" He shrugs. "The best I can be, considerin' that my partner and best friend from school just died. I still don't know how to help his family. There's no fixin' their problems, but I could spend some time with Georgie. Mario couldn't wait to play catch and teach him how to ride a bike. Those are things I can do for him, if Lauren wants. It's not much, but I want to be there for them."

My sweet boy—he's always so thoughtful and a great friend. I squeeze his arm. "Those are big things, and I just know Lauren and Connie will be grateful."

Julia Caroline leans forward from the backseat. "I agree. You are such a wonderful young man. You being around will make a huge difference in Georgie's life."

Clint's cheeks redden. He's never been one to brag on

himself or enjoy when others celebrate him or something he's done. I'm glad he's humble, but he needs to learn how to appreciate a little praise from time to time.

His forehead wrinkles—*what is on his mind?* I am reluctant to press him, so I sit back and look out the window. The palmetto tree fronds sway in the breeze. A walk along the beach is in order today. I need to unwind, and Vitamin Sea is the best medicine for my soul.

"Gram?"

"Yes, hon?"

"When Georgie screamed for Mario, it was almost like he saw him. But that isn't possible … is it?"

I sigh. "You know my thoughts on the matter. I've often seen and heard things that others don't, and you saw your mama when you were a little boy. Do you remember that?"

"I don't. But if you say I did, I reckon I believe you." He gulps. "Have you seen Mario?"

My jaw drops. I didn't expect this question from him. He is level-headed and never leans into the spiritual world beyond going to church, praying, and reading the Bible. Since he was little, I've explained that there are countless things on this earth we don't understand yet, but God has a plan. It's our job to trust Him.

Julia Caroline pokes my shoulder. "Answer the boy."

Shaking myself out of my thoughts, I swallow hard. "Sorry. I'm just in shock. You never talk about ghostly things. Why the change of heart?"

He pulls on his shirt collar. "Georgie was so insistent that he saw Mario. I know kids make up stories and can have big imaginations, but he's too little to understand how to lie. I haven't really seen you talking to ghosts, that I remember anyway. It's different when you witness someone experiencing it firsthand. Suddenly, it seems more real. Does that make sense?"

"It does, hon. And to answer your question from earlier—I saw Mario at the hospital. I didn't recognize him … it had been so long since I'd seen him, and our ghostly reunion was completely unexpected."

I explain everything that has happened to this point. This must be difficult for Clint, but his facial expression doesn't change much except for his eyes widening a couple of times. His police officer training helps him keep his cool in all situations. Are officers trained on how to react if they see a ghost or something else otherworldly?

Surely, some officers have encountered the unexplainable. A few probably even bear the same gift ... er, curse ... as Julia Caroline and me.

I wouldn't wish this blasted connection with the Other Side on my worst enemy, but I suppose clairvoyance helps sometimes. It's only brought me heartache and pain to this point, especially when my ex-husband's vengeful spirit decided to make a grand entrance right after my son and daughter-in-law, Clint's parents, died in a horrible car accident.

If Julia Caroline hadn't walked me through the chaos, I don't know what I would have done. Her father-in-law's death and haunting awakened her abilities when we were younger. Tragedy often sparks this particular gift in many people. Your heart is in such a vulnerable state that your mind is willing to accept seeing and hearing new things, whether your brain wants to or not.

Poor Georgie lost his daddy and is too young to understand that this new version of Mario isn't of this world.

Whether they've experienced horrific events, children tend to be more receptive to seeing and communicating with spirits and usually outgrow it as they mature. I hope this is the case for him. No one needs to be haunted by the constant chatter of ghosts everywhere they go, be scared to death when someone randomly pops up beside them in their car, or have ghosts ask for an endless slew of favors. It's exhausting.

Shaking myself out of my thoughts, I peer out the Jeep

window—we're parked in my driveway. *How long have we been here?* I lost track of time and place before we left Connie's.

I pull myself together and pat Clint's shoulder. "Hon, you want to come in for some peach cobbler and ice cream? I'm going to cook up some food to take over to Connie and Lauren. If you want to stay, I can send some home with you, too. I'm so used to cooking for an army … I don't know how to cook for a handful of people."

Clint puts out his hand. "No. Thanks. I need to go. The guys and I have been texting all afternoon. We're going to find whoever killed Mario."

My heart twists up in knots. I understand why he wants to find this person, but then, what? *Will they target Clint? What if they are already following him?* I shudder. I want someone else to figure out who could have committed such a crime. But this is his duty—there's no stopping him from pursuing the monster. I have to respect that.

Ignoring the nausea twitching in my belly, I lean over and kiss his cheek. "I love you. Be extra careful and let me know when you're back home and safe. I'll be praying for you boys."

Julia Caroline blows him a kiss, and we both get out of the Jeep.

As he backs out of the driveway, I push back tears. Having a police officer in the family isn't for the faint of heart. He is so good at his job, and it wouldn't be fair to ask him to change careers. It's all he's ever wanted to do, just like his daddy.

Wesley would be proud to see Clint in action, serving and protecting our wonderful little island. No doubt about that.

Julia Caroline pulls me by the hand. "C'mon. We've gotta make a mess of shrimp and cheesy grits for Connie and 'em. Little Georgie is a growing boy. We need to keep their bellies full while they're grieving. Lord knows we've both been there."

She ain't wrong.

I unlock the front door, and we go back to the kitchen. Julia Caroline pulls all the ingredients out of the fridge and preps the shrimp and veggies for sautéing while I boil broth for the grits. The divine scents of a proper Lowcountry kitchen infiltrate every square inch of the space.

My stomach growls—*yum*—I'll never tire of this amazing aroma.

While the grits thicken, I pull a peach cobbler I made last week out of the freezer to thaw. Connie can warm it up when they're ready to dig into a heaping plate of the comforting goodness.

Julia Caroline mixes some heavy cream and two generous spoonfuls of my homemade pimento cheese into the grits, then pours the mixture into a casserole dish. I top it with the shrimp and sauteed veggies, add a thin drizzle of barbecue sauce, and secure the lid.

We load dinner and dessert into my car. Connie's house is just around the corner, but I'm not coordinated enough to carry this much food without dropping it. Julia Caroline doesn't even question my thought process. She knows my clumsy ways too well. We don't need another fine mess.

I drive the short block and a half to Connie's house and sigh as I park. *Is today real?* Perhaps I'll wake up and realize it's all been a horrible nightmare. Mario was taken much too young. *Why do these painful events happen?*

I try not to question God, but it's difficult to wrap my noggin around why someone dies before they've lived a full life.

It's no wonder Mario's spirit is lingering here. Even though Heaven sounds like a dream come true, it would be devastating to leave your young child and beautiful wife behind. I couldn't have left Wesley or his children behind when they were Georgie's age.

Nope ... my ghostly rear end would have stayed planted smack dab in the middle of this island, haunting my poor babies to make sure no harm came their way.

CHAPTER 7

When we arrive back at Connie's place, we unload the comfort food smorgasbord. The scents mingle with the salty air, creating an intoxicating blend. My stomach rumbles at the thought of devouring a helping of creamy grits.

As I ring the doorbell, the tiny hairs on the back of my neck stand on end. *Is someone watching me?* I peer out the corner of my eye but don't see a soul—alive or dead.

Just then, Julia Caroline nudges me. "We've got company."

Mario is standing beside the porch. I almost drop my casserole dish. You would think I'd be used to these surprise visits by now. But I reckon it isn't exactly normal to see or converse with the dead, even if you've encountered hundreds of ghosts.

Connie will open the door any second now. *How am I supposed to talk to Mario without her thinking I've lost my ever-loving mind?*

I turn to Julia Caroline. "After I say hi to Connie, I'm going back to the car for a minute. Anyone who wants to chat with me should follow me over there."

She winks at me and nods. Thank goodness, she gets me and my bizarre thought process.

A moment later, Connie answers the door, and I hand her the casserole dish, saying I have one more thing to grab. Julia Caroline follows her inside, and I wander back over to the car. I have no idea what to retrieve from the trunk that will make sense, but I'll figure it out.

When I reach the back of the car, Mario materializes in a silvery veil.

Just in case anyone is watching me, I rummage through the contents of my trunk to give the appearance of searching for a specific item.

"Hon, I don't have too long before your mama comes to check on me. How can we help you prepare for crossing over to the Other Side? You deserve to rest and not worry about worldly things."

Mario shakes his head. "Nothing will make me okay with leaving my family. Who is going to make sure they have everything they need?"

I suck in a deep breath. "It isn't the same, but we'll do everything we can to support them. Clint wants to be there for Georgie, and I'm not sure if your mama has told you, but she spends a lot of holidays with Julia Caroline and me. Your family will always be welcome in our homes. We 'll never say no to having more loved ones in our lives."

Mario smiles. "Thank you. That helps a lot." His brow furrows, and he turns paler—quite the feat for a ghost. "There's just one problem. I didn't see the person who shot me, but I have my suspicions. He's the reason we left San Diego."

The front door swings open, and Connie leans her head out. "Hey. You'd better hurry in here. I'm not gonna be able to keep Georgie away from this peach cobbler much longer. I'm tempted to dive into the dish headfirst myself."

"Be right there!" What in the heck can I take inside with me? A pack of store-bought snickerdoodle cookies catches my eye.

They must have fallen out of my grocery bag when I did my shopping earlier this week. *Thank goodness!* When Connie closes the door, I tell Mario to come by my house in a couple of hours. Maybe he has information that will help Clint put the sorry loser behind bars.

Snickerdoodles in hand, I close the trunk and let myself into Connie's house.

"Sorry about that. I wanted Georgie to have these cookies." I despise lying, but it's necessary this time.

"Thank you both for taking care of my family. I don't know what we'd do without you right now." Connie's voice shook at the end, tugging at my heart. *I absolutely hate that she is going through this.*

I take her hand. "We love you. Anytime you need us, just say the word. Now, let's fix Georgie a plate, so we can all enjoy a massive slab of cobbler."

While we eat, I try to steer the conversation away from topics involving Mario or the police department. I'm not the best at keeping secrets. I'm afraid of slipping up and mentioning that I saw Mario. That will only bring confusion and pain to their family. Thankfully, Georgie is chattering away nonstop about dinosaurs. I only understand every few words, but he's so happy. I just smile and nod when it seems appropriate.

After we finish our meal, I stretch and yawn. "I don't know about y'all, but that cobbler sent me over the edge. I need to go home and rest these weary, old eyes."

Julia Caroline and I say our goodbyes and hug everyone, promising to check on them in the morning. I don't like leaving Connie in this fragile state, but at least she isn't alone. Lauren and Georgie will help keep her spirits up.

When we're back in the car, I tell Julia Caroline about my chat with Mario.

Her eyes widen. "What are you waiting for? We'd better go back to your house."

As we make the short drive home, I wonder who Mario

suspects shot him. Who would harm such a wonderful young man? Connie has always been so proud of how he and Lauren volunteered with their church in San Diego, and Mario coached Georgie's tiny tot soccer team. They had a lot of friends and had built a found family in their community.

Wait ... was it someone Mario arrested? That has to be it. It's such a shame that anyone would go that far to get revenge, but it wouldn't be surprising.

The moment I park my car in the driveway, the faint silvery outline of a person shimmers on my front lawn. I squint ... *is that Mario?* Julia Caroline, and I get out of the car and run toward the fading aura. My pulse is beating out of control.

I swallow hard. "Mario, is that you? Please come back!" I wait for a minute, but he doesn't return. My heart sinks—*we didn't make it back in time.*

Julia Caroline frowns. "Out of all the dumb luck. Sometimes the recently deceased don't have much control over how long they stay in one place, especially if it isn't their home or where they died."

"Blast it all! I should have just talked to him at Connie's."

"Nan, don't beat yourself up. You couldn't have a deep, lengthy conversation with him over there. What if someone had overheard you?"

I cover my face with my hands. "What can I do now? We need to find out who Mario suspects so Clint can take them in for questioning. I'm fit to be tied. I want to see them do their time for taking someone's life, especially a young police officer. He was just trying to raise a family and protect his community."

"I'm sure Mario will come back as soon as he can. Just be patient. Let's make a pot of coffee. C'mon."

We go inside and head back to the kitchen. If these walls could talk, they'd have some interesting tidbits to share. They've heard Julia Caroline and I fret over so many problems, mostly conundrums involving ghosts. But they've also witnessed us celebrating wonderful moments, usually over a piece of pie and a warm cup of comforting coffee or tea.

Julia Caroline's face is pale and drawn. My shoulders drop. Today has been such a whirlwind that I haven't slowed down to think about my best friend's health.

"With all the craziness, we haven't talked about what the doctor told you this morning. Should I be concerned? We both know I'm gonna worry, but do I need to be extra worried? Please tell me you're okay."

Julia Caroline sighs. "I told ya, I don't know anything yet. I wasn't lying earlier."

"Well, you'd better tell me when you do."

"Dang it all, woman! I haven't kept any secrets from you in our sixty years of friendship. I couldn't even if I wanted to. You'd pry it from my lips so fast; it would hurt more than any illness ever could." She pauses. "I think it's time for both of us to relax. Do you want me to stay over in case Mario comes back? I can crash in your guest bedroom."

I shake my head. "That's alright. I'll text you if he shows up."

Please, Lord, let Mario come back soon! And while I'm praying for favors, please help my best friend stay healthy!

Julia Caroline hugs me goodbye. "I love you, Nan. I'm going to be okay."

I wish I could be so sure.

CHAPTER 8

For the next week, we take food to Connie's house every day. Around these parts, it's what we do. No mourning Southerner with a tight group of friends will ever starve. Little by little, Connie and Lauren seem a little better rested and nourished. The only negatives are that Clint hasn't gotten any leads on a murder suspect, and Julia Caroline and I ain't seen hide nor hair of Mario. *It's more than a little concerning.*

If Julia Caroline is right about an evil spirit holding him captive, we have to figure out who they are and why they're harassing him.

I've never heard of a ghost being haunted, but it sounds like a miserable existence.

Staying up late has never been on my bucket list. But after I delivered dinner to Connie and Lauren, I returned home and settled into my oversized wingback chair to research hauntings online. I need to find a way to draw out the malevolent spirit and send him away for good, but that's always difficult.

While we work out a more permanent fix, we can send this devil to a temporary holding place. That will free Mario from the spirit's grasp for at least a few hours, giving him a chance to check on his family or even move on to the Other Side for good if he's ready.

I think back to the last scary haunting Julia Caroline and I faced. Until we worked out a permanent fix, we used our endless knowledge of Bible verses and cross jewelry to send the ghosties into a holding place. I retrieve my pendant from my jewelry box and put it in my purse for safekeeping. You can't be too prepared when it comes to unsettled spirits.

At 2:30 a.m., I force myself to stop scrolling on the internet. As I pull on my pajamas and climb into bed, I yawn. *Man—I'm going to sleep all day!*

I wake to the sound of a car pulling into my driveway and check the time on my alarm clock—9 o'clock. It's a little later than I usually sleep, but it's also pretty dang early for anyone to come over unannounced.

I pull on my robe and slippers and run to open the front door. Clint's Jeep is parked in the driveway.

Why is he here so early, and where did he go? I don't want to walk around the yard without getting dressed first. The last thing I need is to fall and for the neighbors to see my white satin bloomers under my flowered nightgown. *That wouldn't be a win for anyone. Nope.*

I go back inside to get dressed and pull a comb through my hair. After I'm presentable, I run to the kitchen to put on a pot of coffee and toast some cinnamon crumble muffins.

I hear the front door open and call out to Clint. "I'm in the kitchen, hon. Come on back."

When he reaches the kitchen, his face is crestfallen, his eyes bloodshot. *Ugh—he hasn't slept much either. My poor guy.* It kills me when any of my boys are suffering.

"I know you're hurting. Have a seat, and I'll pour us some coffee while you tell me what you're chawing on right now."

"Gram, I'm torn up over this whole situation. We have no idea how to find the shooter. We've dug through interstate camera footage and put out a press release with a call for witnesses to come forward. If no one does, though, how are we going to figure out who he is?"

I share what Mario told me at Connie's and about our bad timing.

Clint sighs. "Life is so dang frustrating. There wasn't anything you could do."

"I hope he'll come back, but there's no way to predict when he might show up. I'm going to hang out close to the house, just in case." I bite my lip. "I hate to ask when you're preoccupied, but would you mind taking a chicken casserole and some biscuits over to Connie and Lauren later today?"

"Sure. I'm not planning to work unless we find a lead."

"Thanks, hon. I'll call and check on her in a little bit and let her know you'll be by in a bit. So, no luck finding anything?"

He wrings his hands. "Nope. The guys are digging for clues, but it isn't lookin' good."

"I hope you find 'em, but remember—no matter the outcome—this is in God's hands. Everyone has to pay their due. Karma always comes back around on earth, and they'll be judged for their actions on the Other Side."

Clint nods. "Yep. You ain't wrong. We're gonna do our best to find them, though. Do you need some help cookin' for Connie?"

How thoughtful of him to ask! I kiss Clint's forehead and put him to work boiling rice and broccoli as I thaw out a deboned chicken I cooked last week. When we're both finished, we combine everything in a casserole dish with cream of mushroom soup, then top it with cracker crumbs and celery salt before popping it into the oven.

We sit down to play a hand of cards. Neither of us is into the game at first, but after Clint beats me by sheer luck in the second round, my competitive drive kicks in. I throw down a killer hand.

"You'd best be glad we ain't playing for money, hon!"

Clint laughs. "I guess so. But don't forget you're talking to an officer of the law."

I smirk. "You'd have to take me away kicking and screaming. It's been ages since we've sat down to play a game. We need to play cards more often, and your brothers are overdue for a visit. We'll have to challenge that rowdy bunch to a round or two soon."

A chilly breeze grazes the back of my neck, sending a tingle down my spine. That's odd, considering we're in the tropics, and I have the oven cranked to 450. I perk up. *Is Mario about to appear?* Clint stares at me, but I don't say anything. I can't get this poor boy's hopes up again. What can I do to coax the spirit out of hiding without being obvious?

The oven timer buzzes, and I hide my smile—*perfect timing!*

After I wrap the dish in a kitchen towel, I put it inside a thermal bag to keep it warm. My grandmother would have called these newfangled bags magical, and she wouldn't have been wrong! Clint hugs me, grabs the dish, and heads over to Connie's house to deliver their dinner.

Whew! Boy, I'm glad I didn't have to come up with a clever way to get rid of Clint. In my old age, I'm running out of genius ideas.

As soon as the Jeep backs out of the driveway, I call out for Mario.

"Hon, can you show yourself? We're here alone, so you don't have to worry. I just want to help Clint figure out who killed you, so we can make them pay for their crime. Please come see me. I'm not leaving my house today."

I pace the kitchen, and the ceramic floor tiles cool my aching feet. This getting old business ain't for sissies. But that's okay because I'm a tough old crow.

While walking around, I daydream about how much I love my home. It may not have all the modern conveniences of the new constructions popping up in Mount Pleasant, but I don't care. I adore the worn wooden floors and the hand-carved mantle, hewn by Julia Caroline's late husband, James. Those two were a match made in Heaven if there ever was one.

I never had a romance like that. It's too late now, and that's fine by me. I have all my grandsons.

Something catches my eye as I pass by my bedroom window. An iridescent haze shimmers beside my potting shed. I run through the house to the kitchen, knocking over a pile of clean, folded shirts off the ottoman in the living room on the way. *No matter. It's not going anywhere. Why can't I convince a ghost to put away the laundry, just once?*

By the time I make it outside, the haze has disappeared. I let out a low, guttural growl. *Dang it! How am I ever gonna catch up with Mario?*

I sit down on the bench in my garden and notice an odd pattern in the sand below my feet. *Well, I'll be!* The squiggles appear to spell a name or a word. I can clearly make out "Da," but the last letter is unfinished … like someone or something interrupted whoever wrote this. I scratch my head. *Good golly, who wrote that, and what does it mean?*

"Mario, did you try leaving me a note? I need more information to help you. Please come back!"

A flock of seagulls passes overhead, answering me with their annoying call.

"Who asked y'all anything, you silly birds?" I wave my fist as they squawk back at me. I've never been a fan of birds. On the island, they're everywhere I go and getting into everything I own, not to mention the mess they make. If I had a dollar for every time I've cleaned up their nasty poop, I'd be rolling in it … money that is.

"Caw, caw, yourselves—now scat!" They fly off toward the beach, and I jump up and down. "Goodbye and good riddance!"

"Gram, what on earth are you doing?" I turn to see Clint standing at the kitchen door, wearing a sheepish grin. *Oh, good Lord. He must think I've slid off my rocker. What bad timing!*

"Why are you yellin' at those birds? What did they do to

you?" I start to explain, but I giggle and can't stop. Tears spring out of my eyes, which makes me laugh harder. I must seem like a nut to this boy. When I finally catch my breath, I pull a handkerchief and wipe my eyes.

"I'm sorry, hon. I have a bone to pick with them, preferably a wishbone." He shakes his head but cracks a smile. "I'm glad you're laughing like that. It's been a while."

"We've had a lot on our plates lately. Like I said earlier, we're overdue for some family fun. Why don't you ask your brothers when they can visit next, or we can meet them somewhere else. I'd just love to spend a weekend with all my boys. It doesn't matter where."

Clint nods. "That would be awesome. But I still want to focus on helping Connie and Lauren. They must be missing Mario somethin' fierce. I could tell they'd been crying. Georgie was napping, so I didn't talk too much."

"You're right. They need us; we're the only family they have 'round here. Speaking of Mario, look at what I found."

Frowning, I show him the squiggles in the sand and ask what he thinks.

Clint's jaw drops. "Was Mario trying to write, 'Dad?' He couldn't have meant his pa. Coach Rodriguez wouldn't cause anyone a lick of harm. He was a good Christian man."

Connie's late husband and Mario's father was the high school football coach and would give the shirt off his back to a complete stranger. Everyone on the island treasured him, and he loved them back.

I shiver. "What if it's Lauren's dad? I mean, we don't know him."

Clint grimaces and kicks the ground. "Dang it all! It's always someone close to the woman who kills the husband. Usually, it's the husband who kills the wife, but that's a whole other story."

Holy moly! I've got to call Julia Caroline!

CHAPTER 9

I run to the phone and steady my shaking hands. *Just breathe.* I need my best friend's brilliant brain to help us figure out a plan of attack for this haunting. Obviously, we'll let Clint handle any police business, but she always has creative ideas for getting out of the most complicated scrapes. *What in the devil is going on? Hopefully, she'll have an opinion.*

Drawing a deep breath, I dial Julia Caroline's number and play with the curly phone cord. Clint makes fun of me for insisting on keeping a landline. Call me crazy, but I don't like having my darn cell phone turned on all the time. No one needs to be that reachable.

When she answers, I cut her off. "C'mon over! We have a lead, but I'm not sure what to make of it."

Where did Clint go? I got so excited I didn't notice him leave.

I start a pot of coffee and pull some cinnamon rolls from the freezer to thaw. If I know us, we'll be talking for quite a while, which always makes us work up a healthy appetite for junk food.

I hear the front door crack open and start to walk that way.

"Gram? Where are ya? Julia Caroline's here."

"In the kitchen. Why don't y'all come sit with me for a spell? We've got a lot to figure out."

They both join me at the table, and I pour each of us a big, piping hot cup of coffee. I catch Julia Caroline up on everything.

She slaps her face. "Oh, my word! Do you really believe Lauren's dad would kill Mario? Are we jumping to conclusions here?"

I tilt my head. "We just met her, and we hadn't seen Mario for ten years or longer. Who's to say he didn't get mixed up in something shady? Not that I think that's the case, and I'd hope he didn't marry into any craziness. But you never can tell for sure."

Clint smacks the table, shaking the floor underneath. "No way! Mario wouldn't have done anything to jeopardize his family's safety. I don't think Lauren would either, but I don't know her dad."

"Hon, don't take it personally. We're just trying to figure out what happened to your friend. We want to help."

Clint swallows hard and looks at the ceiling. "I'm going to run a background check on Lauren's dad. I pray we don't find a lick of evidence against him." He pauses. "Lauren and Georgie have already been through hell. They don't need to deal with nothin' else."

I nod and look over at Julia Caroline. "Do you have any ideas for how we can send this beast who's harassing Mario to the Other Side?"

"My family's pearls have some powerful magic in them. We add a pearl every time someone has a baby, gets married, or loses a loved one. That's what makes them so mystical. But all the conditions have to be right for them to work. We'd have to wait for a full moon, among other things."

She stops talking. Her face scrunches, and she goes pale. *That's odd.*

"What's the matter? Is someone behind me?"

I turn around, hoping Mario is waiting to chat with us.

Instead, a loud thud reverberates from across the table. I look back over, and Julia Caroline is slumped over the table.

Please, God, help her! I jump up and run over to my best friend, knocking my chair over in the process. Her breathing is labored but steady. Clint takes her pulse and tells me to call 911. Pushing back tears, I dial the number and ask him what I should say to the dispatcher.

"Gram, tell 'em her pulse is a little high, but nothin' too awful. I'm pretty sure she just blacked out, but better safe than sorry."

After I hang up the phone, I run to Julia Caroline and shake her shoulder.

"Please, hon, we need you to wake up. You hit your head, but you're gonna be just fine. The paramedics are on their way."

She groans, blinks, and starts to lift her head, but Clint stops her.

"Hold it! Stay put, just in case you bumped your head harder than we think. Can you tell me your name and where you live?"

"I'm Julia Caroline Mason, and I live on Palm Court, the most exquisite street on Isle of Palms ... same place I've lived your whole life ... most of my life, for that matter. I'm not senile yet, young man."

Clint smirks. "That's exactly what I was hoping you'd say. You're definitely going to have a bruise on your noggin in the morning, but I think you'll be okay. To be safe, keep your head as still as possible. The EMTs will be here soon."

I pull a chair up next to Julia Caroline. "If you wanted to lie down, you should have just gone to the guest room to nap. No need for all the grand theatrics."

"Hush, you old cow." She stares at me out of the corner of her eye, and I cackle. She starts to giggle, shaking her head against the table.

I can't stop cackling. We're never content to let a tense situation get the best of us. Clint puts an end to our fun. "Hey, cut it out, you two. She needs to hold still—this might be more serious than it looks." I bite my lip and avoid making eye contact with Julia Caroline. We can't help ourselves. It doesn't matter that we're in our sixties. Growing up is overrated.

Sirens wail, and red lights shimmer into the house through the living room window. Clint jumps to his feet to open the front door for the paramedics.

They run inside and follow him into the kitchen. As they examine Julia Caroline, I hold my breath. On the surface, she seems okay, but she blacked out for a reason. *Is this connected to the tests the hospitals ran?* I try to push the negativity out of my mind. Until we receive the test results, we won't know what, if anything, is wrong.

Please, Lord, protect this incredible woman.

The EMTs ask Julia Caroline a series of questions. After a few minutes, they recommend that she go with them to the hospital. My stomach lurches as she looks at Clint for his opinion.

He huffs. "Dang it all, woman. Just go get checked out. What does it hurt?"

She sighs but nods, and the paramedics help her onto a gurney. A cold chill creeps down my spine, and I attempt to shake it off. Bless it all, this is the last thing I needed today. I stay one step behind the EMTs as they push Julia Caroline out of the house and load her into the ambulance.

I turn back to Clint. "I'm going with her."

"No surprises there. I'll follow y'all."

The EMT helps me up into the ambulance, and I sit down close to Julia Caroline.

I grab her hand. "Everything's gonna be okay."

She rolls her eyes. "Duh—I'm just going to the hospital because you and Clint would never let it go if I didn't."

"Glad you've finally decided to give in to reason. I don't know why it took so long!"

Out of the corner of my eye, I spy a silver shimmering aura materializing on the front porch. Doesn't that beat all? The very moment I can't talk to Mario, he shows up on my doorstep. It will just have to wait. Julia Caroline's well-being is more important.

I text Clint: Hey, Mario is standing on my front porch. Do you mind trying to talk to him before you leave for the hospital? Even if you can't see him, he can hear you.

Clint: *On it.*

As the ambulance backs out of the driveway, I watch Clint sit down in a rocking chair. He lays his hands on his lap and starts talking. Can he see Mario?

I wish I could see Mario's face, but he is facing Clint, with his back turned toward the road. My heart aches for both of them. Not only has Clint lost his partner and best friend, but he also doesn't believe in ghosts. And here he is talking to a spirit about murder suspects. Mario had someone in mind. *Did he guess it was his father-in-law?*

I gulp. *Did Lauren know, too? What a horrific thought!*

My blood runs cold. Your parents are supposed to go to the ends of the earth to make sure you're safe—no matter what. When you find your true love, they become an extension of you. How could a parent bring harm to such an important person in their child's life? That's the very definition of a narcissist—someone who wants to keep you for themselves and doesn't want you to flourish in your own life unless it somehow benefits them.

I hope we're wrong! Lauren needs all the support she can get. With her mom not being around, her dad should help carry the weight of the world for her and Georgie. Julia Caroline and I will do our darnedest to take away her and Connie's burdens, too.

Speaking of my pal, I've got to focus on her. What if her blacking out isn't a coincidence? We need her bloodwork results.

Once we know she's okay, I'll breathe easier again.

CHAPTER 10

When we arrive at the hospital, the paramedics wheel Julia Caroline into the emergency room. She has them in stitches with her jokes. You wouldn't know she nearly passed out and scared the ever lovin' beejeezus out of Clint and me.

I'm glad she's in good spirits, and I don't mean ghosts. Other than Mario, we don't need any hitchhikers begging for our attention today. They'd better find another clairvoyant sucker to help them. I don't mind when our plates aren't so full. It's part of having this gift, or curse, but we have a whole dang buffet of problems without some needy tagalong butting in and distracting us.

The paramedics leave us in a holding area for a couple of minutes and return with a young blond nurse. She admits Julia Caroline as an emergency room patient and slaps a hospital bracelet onto her wrist before pushing the gurney behind a privacy curtain.

After covering Julia Caroline with a thin, worn blanket, the nurse tells us the doctor will stop by as soon as possible. Then, the nurse slides the curtain aside and ducks out of the room.

I pick up Julia Caroline's hand and smile. "Hey! At least you got a new fashionable bracelet out of all this."

Julia Caroline smirks. "Right? My granddaughters would be so jealous. Don't you think?"

"For sure, especially Blake. She's such a fashion plate. Speaking of your family, do you want me to call them and ..."

She slaps my shoulder. "Heavens, no! Not yet. There's nothing to tell them. All it would accomplish is cause a panic, and I don't want that. They have busy lives and don't need to worry about the likes of little old me. Besides, I'm too tough to die."

I smile weakly. "I know you don't want anyone makin' a fuss over you, but promise me you will tell them after you have the results. I don't like keepin' secrets from those girls. It's been hard enough not telling them they might be cursed with this dad-burned gift of communicating with the dead. I agree with you—they don't need to know yet, but one day, they're going to hear or see a ghost. Someone's gonna have to explain how all this nonsense works to them."

"And if I'm not around, you'll be the one to help them figure it out, right?"

My mouth turns dry like it's full of gooey pluff mud, straight from the salty marsh. When I finally swallow, I choke. I take a swig of water.

Ahh ... my throat is open enough to talk again.

"Hush, woman. You're going to outlive the rest of us."

With ghosts on my mind, I have to wonder why Mario hasn't returned to us. There ain't nothing I despise more than a dead person who is stuck on this planet and wants my help but won't show their darn face. But the Mario Rodriguez I knew wouldn't play games with us, so why can't we see him? Julia Caroline has been haunted by nearly every kind of haint imaginable, so this is a head-scratcher to say the least.

Someone or something has to be preventing him from

appearing to us on a whim. If he can't tell us who shot him, we're going to have to solve the mystery ourselves.

It's an upsetting conundrum to ponder, but as a police officer, Mario probably arrested many people who might want to take revenge. *Good gravy—would any of them follow him all the way from California to South Carolina?* It seems unlikely, but people are unpredictable at the best of times. Mario's cryptic note etched into the sand in my garden made it look like he might suspect his father-in-law was to blame. As much as I hate to bother a grieving widow, we're going to need to find a delicate way to approach Lauren and pick her brain.

I wish I'd gotten to know her better before asking such horrific questions about her family. Not only did she just lose her husband and the father of cute little Georgie, but now her dad might be the one responsible for bringing all this sadness and grief? *How do I broach this topic?*

It's not like I can pour her a tall glass of sweet tea to make the conversation less maddening. No amount of sugar or even my divine homemade peach syrup will make what I have to say easier to swallow.

Clint's police training might come in handy. He's wearing a brave face right now, but he's such a young officer. It has to be tough for him to lose one of his few partners in his brief career. I should bow out and let him take Lauren aside. It's part of his job, after all. But as a grandmother, I want to protect him at all costs.

Julia Caroline waves her hand in front of my face, and I smack it out of the way.

"What in the heck are you doin'? Your mama taught you better—it's rude to put your hand in someone's face."

She scrunches her nose. "Um, you're looking mighty spacey right now. I was just bringing you back to the land of the living."

I scowl. "Do you have any bright ideas for how to ask Lauren about her dad? I'm trying to think through all this hullabaloo, so we don't send her runnin' back to San Diego. It's not something I ever thought I'd talk about with Connie's daughter-in-law."

Julia Caroline shrugs. "All we can do is try to be supportive. Surely, she wants to know who killed her husband. If we can help both her and Mario's spirit get closure, it will all be worthwhile. Mario deserves to rest in peace, and Lauren and Georgie need to find some normalcy on this godforsaken planet."

Poor Lauren and Mario. They should have had a beautiful life together with their children. They deserve to have a dad around as they grow up. Connie should have had many years left with her boy, too. It isn't fair. I reckon nothing is, though.

My Wesley and his lovely MaryAnne should still be here, reveling in how wonderful their sons turned out. I couldn't be prouder of these young men. Speaking of which, I need to talk to Clint about Lauren. So, I texted him asking him to come to the hospital. We've gotta get this plan going, so all of us can rest without tossing and turning all night.

While Julia Caroline and I wait for him to show up, a nurse comes into the room and draws blood from her arm. I shiver. Needles aren't my favorite, but we've gotta find out why she fainted earlier today. The stress of Mario's murder and the mystery surrounding our so-called gift of clairvoyance is getting to both of us.

Nothing is seriously wrong with Julia Caroline, right? Surely, we have at least a couple more decades of raising Cain together.

The walls of the small examination room seem to draw closer by the minute. My palms are sweating like nobody's business. One way or another, we have to bust out of here.

Julia Caroline cracks jokes with everyone who enters the room.

How does she stay so calm about her health? I guess I'm worried enough for both of us.

When Clint arrives, I ask him to go somewhere we can talk in private.

Before we leave, I look back at my best friend. "Call me the second a doctor comes in, and I'll come right back. Got it?"

She salutes me. "Yes, ma'am."

I shake my head and follow Clint through the winding hallways, past the gift shop and cafeteria, to a set of double doors that lead to a courtyard. Spanish moss streams down the grand oaks in the center of the brick-walled garden.

Clint sits down on a wrought-iron bench and sighs. "The past couple of weeks have been so dang aggravating and painful. I was so stoked when Mario said he was moving back. We had so many plans to help families who live on the island. This summer, we were going to coach a soccer team for at-risk youth and collect toys from local businesses for the kids at Christmas. It doesn't seem real that he's gone."

My heart aches for my boy. I pat his back. "I'm so sorry, hon. It's been terrible. I know you haven't seen any spirits before, but did you see Mario back at my house? He was standing there as the ambulance pulled away."

Clint shakes his head. "I wish I could have. I don't know if he could hear me, but I tried to tell him we want to help—if he can stick around your house, we'll be back as soon as we can." He wipes the corner of his eye.

"We need to talk to Lauren, but I have no idea how to start that conversation about her dad. What do you think?"

He grimaces. "It's all I've been able to think about. I'm dreading it, but we have no choice. Before I can say anything, I'd have to clear it with the Chief, and I don't think he'd go for it without more reasonable cause than finding some random letters written in the sand. I hate to ask, but can you talk to her? I think she'd take it better from you, anyway."

"I'm not sure what to say. I don't want to offend her, or she won't want us around anymore. I can't exactly march over to Connie's to tell them I've seen Mario, and he's trying to send me a message from the Other Side. What do you suggest?"

Clint gives me some pointers on how to question family

members gently. *Ugh. I can't believe I'm doing this, but first things first—we have to bust Julia Caroline out of this joint.* I brace my hands on the bench to pull myself up and groan along with my knees. This getting old business is tougher than a two-dollar steak, but it beats the alternative.

"I'll do my best talking to Lauren tonight. C'mon. Let's go check on Julia Caroline."

We wander the halls back to the examination room. A doctor wearing a bowtie and horn-rimmed spectacles reaches the doorway at the same time. He grabs the clipboard right outside the room and looks over his glasses at us.

"Are you Mrs. Mason's family?"

Without thinking, I put my hand on my hip. "I'm her sister, and this is my grandson." I probably shouldn't have layered on the sass, but what can I say … it comes naturally.

"I'm Dr. Bowman." He gives me a skeptical smirk but waves us into the room. "After you."

My heart races as I walk toward Julia Caroline. Doctors don't ask about your relationship unless they have bad news. *Oh, dear Lord, please bless and protect this good woman!*

I sit on the edge of the hospital bed and hold Julia Caroline's hand.

She furrows her brow when my hand shakes hers. "Nan, I could feel your pulse from across the room. You need to calm down; there's nothing to worry about." She looks over at the doctor. "Tell her, Doc—I'm going to be fine, and you're going to send me home, right?"

He clears his throat and flips through her chart. "Mrs. Mason, we're keeping you for observation tonight and more testing. Some results from the tests we ran earlier this week have come back. Your white blood cell count is elevated, well outside the normal range. I recommend resting up here, but try not to fret."

I put out my hand. "Whoa. What are we talking about here—

cancer? She had some melanomas cut out earlier this year. Did they metastasize?"

Unfortunately, I went down a similar road with my mama. She passed from lung cancer that spread to her breasts back in the early 80s. It was heartbreaking, and I can't fathom how much it would hurt to witness Julia Caroline going through the same nightmare.

He grimaces. "We're not ready to make any diagnoses, but it could be serious. We're keeping a close eye on everything. Your sister is in good hands. If anything critical is going on, we'll figure out the next steps together."

The bottom of my stomach drops out, and I hold my breath.

I'd rather face a thousand hitchhiking ghosts on a ten-mile-long, rickety suspension bridge than deal with the thoughts churning through my brain right now. I stare at the ceiling to avoid making eye contact with Julia Caroline and send more prayers up to God. To the universe. To anyone who will listen.

We're gonna need a miracle.

CHAPTER 11

At midnight, the night nurse finally convinces me to leave Julia Caroline's cramped hospital room. Looking over my shoulder at my best friend sleeping, almost tears my soul in two. She seems so fragile lying on the bed.

If James, Julia Caroline's dear husband, were still alive, he would know how to help her. And he would tell me not to worry; he had everything under control.

But he left us ten years ago ... much too soon. They had a special kind of relationship everyone dreams about, but few people experience. If losing the love of her life didn't kill her, what will be powerful enough to zap the life out of the magnificent Julia Caroline Mason?

She's a tough old biddy. That's the only thing reassuring me in this whole mess.

As I drive home, I think through everything I need to accomplish today—rest a bit if that's humanly possible, check on my best friend when visiting hours start, and talk to Lauren about unthinkable things. *Who can sleep with such nonsense taking up space in their head?*

Pulling into my driveway, I see a light turn off inside the house. *What the heck?*

Did a light bulb burn out at that very second? It must have. There aren't any cars parked nearby, and it would be quite the clip for anyone to hoof it from the nearest street parking or public lot.

Should I call Clint? I don't want to wake him over something silly like a bad bulb or worn-out wiring, but what if someone is inside my house? What would anyone want from me or my home? I don't own a bunch of fancy jewelry or newfangled electronics. I ain't never kept big piles of cash or high limit credit cards lying around my place. I reckon they don't know that, but surely, they'll take one look at my old tube TV and realize they'd hit the wrong house.

Grabbing the small mother of pearl handled pistol from my purse, I swallow hard. I don't want to shoot anyone, but I will if it means protecting myself.

I gently open and close my car door and tiptoe to the mudroom door, on the opposite side of the house from where I saw the light. The door is still locked, so no one could have come in this way. I creep quietly into the living room, and the deadbolt is still secure on the front door.

Unless somebody broke a window and crawled through, I'm alone in here. *Whew! I didn't want to send someone to their maker tonight!*

My pulse slows to an almost normal pace as I explore the bedrooms and kitchen and don't find any broken glass, ransacked cupboards, or other signs of intruders. I let out a deep exhale of relief and laugh as I put my gun back in my purse. *Wow ... I'm definitely on edge. It's understandable with all the chaos in my life.*

A good cup of hot tea should help calm my nerves a bit. I put a kettle of water on to boil.

While I'm waiting, I pick up some clutter and wipe down the countertops and table. I'm not a neat freak, but with everything going on, I might not have a chance to clean anytime soon. I don't need an army of ants taking over my kitchen if I neglect it for a few days.

The kettle whistles, and I pour the piping hot water over a bag of my favorite peach black tea from the Charleston Tea Plantation. The plantation is on John's Island, just a hop, a skip, and a jump from here. Julia Caroline and I love spending a morning on the grounds and shopping for other goodies before going to soak up the grandness of the nearby ancient Angel Oak Tree. We always stop at Crosby's Seafood Market at Folly Beach on the way back home. Their shrimp is the freshest and has the richest and saltiest flavor of any I've eaten.

As my cup of tea steeps, I finish cleaning up the kitchen. A loud crash followed by a clanging sound comes from the mudroom, and my arm's hair stands on end. *What the heck?* I eye my purse in the living room and run to grab my gun again.

Dang it! I thought the dramatics were over. Did someone sneak in and hide after all? Slinking toward the side door, I try to steady my breathing. Having a panic attack isn't going to help me stay safe.

I flip the light switch on, ready to shoot if necessary. When my eyes adjust, I see that a large metal laundry basket has fallen off the dryer, sending its contents across the mudroom floor. I roll my eyes at myself. Shooting a plumb worn-out basket ain't gonna help anyone. *Get a grip, Nancy! You can't freak out at every little bump or clank.*

I tuck my pistol into my pocket and bend over to pick up the basket, along with the stack of clean clothes that had been stowed inside, waiting for me to put them away.

Thank goodness I didn't shoot holes into my bras or drawers; that might have been a little drafty and embarrassing this winter. I giggle at the mental image of wearing holey underwear underneath my Sunday best while sitting on the back pew.

It wouldn't have been an appropriate church topic, but it would have been funny and exactly the sort of thing to keep

Julia Caroline and me in stitches during the early morning service. All the proper ladies always stare at us during our fits. Those women need to live a little. Having a stick up your rear-end all the time must be pretty uncomfortable.

The sound of men arguing behind me sends my heart racing again. *Who is that? How did they make it inside with all the blasted doors and windows locked?*

Gently setting the basket on the floor, I grab the pistol from my pocket and pivot to see Mario's apparition reaching for me. Another spirit, a man wearing a blue and white striped baseball cap with the brim yanked down over his eyes, pulls Mario back by his shoulders.

I let out a shrill scream and throw my hands up in the air. "What on God's green earth do you think you're doing to Mario? You leave him alone this instant! You hear me?"

The devilish man sneers at me and keeps his head turned downward. *Is this Lauren's dad?* His hat casts a long shadow over his face; I can't pick out his facial features. From what I can tell, he has dark hair and a deeper complexion—not much to go on in the big scheme of things.

I still can't fathom why Mario's father-in-law would kill him. How did he shoot him if he's dead? And if he isn't around, wouldn't he want Mario to protect and provide for Lauren and Georgie?

That just plain doesn't make a lick of sense.

Wait … Lauren mentioned her dad planning to travel from California to help with Georgie. Surely, she didn't mean the ghostly version of her father was going to visit. I wish I could see this spirit's face.

I haven't ever met Lauren's dad, but I could ask to see some family pictures. That would give me a subtle way to uncover this spirit's identity.

Mario elbows him in the ribs, but the malevolent spirit doesn't loosen his grip. I lunge toward them and grab Mario's hand, pulling him away from the other spirit as hard as I can.

Just when I had almost freed Mario from the other ghost's grasp, they both faded into a silvery, iridescent mist. I punch the air in defeat and let out a guttural shriek.

"Nooooooo!!!!!!!!!!!!!"

Stunned, I fall to my knees and growl. I cannot believe that just happened! How can a spirit kidnap another one and disappear into nothingness? There are so many things I don't understand. I can't help but think about how I failed Mario, and by extension, his entire family.

If Julia Caroline were here, she'd know exactly what to do.

But she isn't—she's at the hospital awaiting God only knows what kind of health news. I gulp. As much as I want to help Mario and his family find peace, I have to make sure I don't lose sight of Julia Caroline's needs either. She wouldn't let me down if our roles were reversed.

"Lord—please spare my loving but cantankerous best friend. I'd be so lost without her sassy self to keep me in check. What will I do if she dies before me? She has so many family members who depend on her, too. Most of all—her granddaughters. This lady is our absolute rock. I'd do anything to save her, and I'm not alone. Just show us what we need to do to keep her healthy."

I lie face down on the ice-cold tile floor, with my folded arms supporting my head, and sob uncontrollably for a few minutes. Strangely, the coolness comforts me a little. I roll over and try to pull myself up, but I can't.

My old butt is stuck down here on the floor, and my darn cell phone is on top of the kitchen table, just out of reach. *Dang it all! This could only happen to me!* I laugh hysterically.

Determined, I sit up just enough to grab a padded cushion off a dining chair and place it under my noggin. Despite enjoying the coolness, I need something thin to cover my arms. It's a matter of comfort. I stretch again and pull the sleeve of a buttery soft cardigan, draped across the back of a chair. *Ahhh— that's better!*

Whoever finds me this way is going to have a good laugh at

my expense. But I won't care. I'll just be glad to get up off the floor because every bone in my body is going to throb like a tank hit me.

I've gotta get some shuteye, no matter how impossible it seems. I try to empty my mind and let my worries roll away, picturing the cascading tide just outside my door, sweeping these problems out to the restless sea. Peace sweeps over my soul as I breathe in and out. The sound of waves crashing along the shoreline doesn't hurt. *Thank God for this small but important blessing. I'll never take my beautiful island home for granted.*

After a while, my exhausted body gives in and falls into a deep, dreamless sleep.

CHAPTER 12

"Gram? Are you alright? Wake up! Hey—talk to me."

I wake to Clint standing over me, pointing a flashlight at my eye. *Oh, dear! He thinks I've had a stroke!*

I'm sure I look a fright with my cardigan on backwards and the chair cushion under my head. I can't stop laughing. This isn't an appropriate time to laugh, and it's very risky, considering I haven't been to the bathroom for hours. The thought of wetting my pants in front of my grandson makes me crack up more, making the threat even more dire.

When I regain my composure, I hold out my hands and ask Clint to help me up off the floor. Clint pulls me to my feet, and I stretch my arms over my head as I lean side to side. Every aching bone in my back pops. *That's what I'm talking about!*

"Thank you! That feels so much better!"

"Now, tell me what in the heck happened, and why it's so dang funny."

"Sure thing … just as soon as I've powdered my nose!"

I almost trip as I run to the bathroom. I need to build upper-body strength so I can pull myself up off the floor and avoid another close call.

When I return to the kitchen, Clint raises his eyebrows at me. I catch the giggles again, start huffing and puffing, and have to sit down.

"Umm … are you OK?"

"Yeppers. It's just that's the fastest I've run since the last time I chased a chicken to wring its neck. That's how we put dinner on our family's plates when I was a girl."

Clint cringes. "I don't need to know all that. How long were you on the floor?"

"Pretty much all night." I glance at the clock on my cellphone. In the name of all that's holy, it's already 10 o'clock! I fill him in on the previous night's events, and he groans.

"Oh, man! I don't like all this creepy hocus-pocus business, but I believe you. What are we gonna do?"

"About Mario?" He nods, and I sigh. "I'm not sure yet. I'm hoping Julia Caroline might have some ideas. After I stop by the hospital, I'll take lunch over to Connie and Lauren. Hopefully, I'll find a gentle way to talk to Lauren about her dad."

"I think that will be best. No need to go through all the paperwork based on a hunch. If we have more proof to give Chief, and he bites, then I'll dig in."

"I'll do what I can. Can you fix a pot of coffee while I get ready?"

He doesn't answer but goes to the cabinet to grab all the fixings, so I head upstairs. A frightening image in the vanity mirror almost causes me to scream. Then, I realize it's me, not a haint. *Wow—I look horrible.*

First things first, I need to calm the gray beasts wrestling on my head, which looks like a couple of rabid raccoons stuck their wet paws in a light socket mid-fight.

A mix of water and gel coaxes this rat's nest into a less ruffled coif. It's not great, but at least my hairdo shouldn't frighten children on the street. I paint my lips a darker shade than usual to detract from my wild do, or I might look crazier. *Whatever works!* I slip on a simple black knit top and a matching pair of crisply pressed linen slacks. A singular silver chain with my cross pendant and leather sandals finish the look.

When I return to the kitchen, Clint hands me a cup of coffee and a piece of toast with a hefty dose of my homemade blackberry freezer jam.

"Eat up. I bet you didn't have dinner after I left the hospital last night, even though you promised you would. You need to keep up your energy if you're going to make it through this long day. Remember what the flight attendants always say, 'Put your own oxygen mask on first.'"

"Thanks, hon. I will try to eat a good lunch today at Connie's. It would be rude and seem weird if I ran my mouth nonstop while they eat."

We chat during breakfast, and I can't help but notice how much better I feel. My blood sugar must have tanked while I was sprawled out on the floor last night.

Clint hugs me and says he needs to head to the station for his shift. I kiss his cheek and send him on his way, but a gnawing sensation pops up in my chest. My heart has been heavier since Mario's murder. I'll never get used to the danger my boy faces every day, but I need to let him live his life.

After cleaning up the kitchen again, I go outside to my car. Something feels off, but I can't put my finger on what's wrong. While driving to the hospital, I don't notice the scenery, cars, or people on the way. I'm sure they were all present, but apparently, my mind isn't.

When I've parked, I send up a prayer for Julia Caroline before heading inside. I hope the doctors have delivered good news and that I can take her home. I'd love nothing more than to fix her a mess of biscuits and gravy and a tall glass of sweet tea. Then, we'd sit on the front porch and send all our worries along with the tide. *Wouldn't that be wonderful?*

As I step onto the elevator, my blood goes cold, and each

hair on the back of my neck stands on end. *Do I have a guest?* At a hospital, death is never far away. I look around, but no one is there.

"Mario, is that you? Julia Caroline and I think someone is keeping you from communicating with us. I saw both of you at my house last night. Don't give up. We're all working to help. Keep trying to visit me when you can."

The elevator door pops open to reveal Dr. Bow Tie, wearing a white lab coat over a three-piece suit with his trademark plaid bow tie. His face turns red, and he clears his throat. "I'll catch the next one … thank you very much."

I point to my ear, pretending to have a Bluetooth earbud in place. "Oh, I'm on a call. I promise I'm not nuts."

Still blushing, he waves me on. "That's okay. You go ahead." *I bet he thinks I'm as batty as all get out! I probably am.* At any rate, I haven't fooled anyone. I close the elevator door and continue to Julia Caroline's room. If I had a dollar for every time a ghost made me look crazy, I'd be a wealthy woman. *What are the odds that Dr. Bow Tie witnessed my insanity?*

The elevator dings, and the door slides open again. Thankfully, there's no sign of the traumatized doctor or anyone else, for that matter. I walk briskly to the minuscule room.

I find Julia Caroline sitting upright in the hospital bed. Her eyes are filled with worry, and her tear-stained cheeks are red and puffy. She's as tough as nails and not one to cry, so she must have gotten some plumb awful news.

My stomach drops. "What did I miss?"

She swallows hard and blinks back tears. "The doctor just stopped by during his rounds. More of my test results came back elevated, showing markers for cancer. He thinks you're right about the melanomas metastasizing."

I gulp. *I didn't want to be right.* "Yeah, but they thought they got everything then, and you'd be fine and dandy."

"Well, Dr. Bowman thinks they might have missed something, and it has spread to my lymph nodes. They're gonna keep me here for a couple of days for more tests. The only good news is they're moving me to a bigger room. I can have an overnight guest stay with me." She puts her head in her hands and sobs. "I'm not done here. I want to be around when my granddaughters graduate from college, start their careers, get married, and have babies. They're such strong girls, they'll be okay without me, but I don't want to miss their big moments."

Oh, God, help! This isn't like my best friend. She is always optimistic and never feels sorry for herself—my heart races. I'm looking for the right words when all I want to do is scream bloody murder. But that wouldn't be ladylike or supportive.

Julia Caroline puts her hands up over her head. "Say something. You haven't stopped running your mouth in the past sixty years. It's making me nervous. Not that it takes much on a day like this."

I sigh but force a weak smile. "You're not gonna miss a single moment with your girls. We're going to make sure you have the best care in the entire state of South Carolina. Scratch that ... the whole country. No matter what it takes, everything will be okay because it's gotta be. Don't you worry about a thing." I lean over and kiss her cheek.

With every fiber of my being, I want to throw a hissy fit, holler, and turn over all the furniture in this blasted building. But my best friend needs me to keep it together, so I will try my darnedest to be a civilized lady. *It's gonna be hard!*

CHAPTER 13

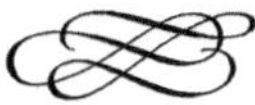

A nurse comes to take Julia Caroline for a battery of tests —an MRI, more blood work, and who knows what else. As she pushes my best friend out of the room in a wheelchair, she tells me this is the perfect time for me to take a break. She also promises to text me when she brings Julia Caroline back to her room.

My heart aches at the thought of leaving my best friend, but I thank her and hug Julia Caroline. "Call if you need anything. I love you, sister."

She turns to blow me a kiss as the wheelchair cuts down the hallway.

I'm relieved to escape the hospital for a while, but I'm not ready to face the tough conversation with Lauren. I rub my chin —this might be my only chance for a few days. I can't blow it.

Steadying my shaking hands, I text Connie to make sure they'll be home. She quickly responds, saying she is fixing lunch, and I should join them on her veranda.

I step back on the elevator and head down to my car. Leaving the hospital parking garage, I head toward the highway and try to perk up a little. Connie and Lauren don't need me bringing them down right now. I'm not telling them the details about Julia Caroline's health yet. We don't know anything for sure, so why borrow trouble when they're already wading through enough pain for a month of Sundays?

Just as I turn onto the Isle of Palms Connector, the overbearing scent of gunpowder overtakes me. My windows are rolled up. Could the air conditioner be pulling in outside smells?

I shrug … maybe some Civil War reenactment group is shooting off cannons at Fort Moultrie on Sullivan's Island today. Crazier things have happened.

A rustling sound coming from the backseat catches my attention, and I glance at my rear-view mirror to see the malevolent spirit who pulled Mario into nothingness waving a gun around. I scream.

What the heck am I supposed to do? There's nowhere to pull over, thanks to a dozen or so bicyclists lining the shoulder of the bridge. I push down the intense fear pulsing throughout my body. I don't have enough time to have a panic attack.

Gulping, I look back and forth between the road and the rear-view mirror. The devil himself gives me a wicked grin while brandishing the pistol.

I'm madder than an old wet hen. "Who are you, and why are you messing with Mario? Did you murder him?"

He scowls. "Now, is that any way to talk to a stranger? I'm wondering exactly who you are and why you care so much about Mario. Maybe I should kill you, too. Whadya say, Grandma—are you ready for the ride of your life? I can send you on a one-way trip Upstairs. It won't hurt for long."

My blood boils, and I smack the steering wheel. "I don't give an opossum's hiney who are. You'd best leave my car. Right now."

I finally gain enough speed to pass the bicyclists and manage to pull over at the end of the bridge. As soon as I throw the car into park, I slip the cross pendant and chain off my neck.

Holding the pendant toward him, I recite the Lord's prayer. When I reach "deliver us from evil," the spirit vanishes into a wispy of silver without leaving so much as a trace of himself behind in my backseat.

Heck yeah! Adrenaline pulses through my veins as I pump my fist in the air. Thankfully, I haven't needed to do that in a while, but it's good to know I've still got what it takes.

I bite my lip. I should have at least gotten his name before sending him away. Hindsight is 20/20. But with these darn malevolent spirits, a cross and a Bible verse aren't enough to keep them away for good. At best, I've got a day to brainstorm a better plan before he comes back to give me more crap.

Weaving through the island to Connie's house, I pray for serenity and grace while talking to Lauren. The good Lord knows I'm only trying to help. I just hope Connie and Lauren see it that way. I don't like butting into other people's business, but I've gotten myself tied up in this drama ... like it or not. *Not* being the keyword.

I sigh as I park in Connie's driveway. *Here goes nothin'.*

Lauren opens the door and hugs me. "Hey! Connie's out back on the veranda setting up. She asked me to watch out for you. It's so great to see you! My mother-in-law is so awesome, and I love her. She's the best grandma to Georgie. But we need some fresh conversation topics."

I laugh. "I understand, hon. You can definitely have too much of a good thing. When you're ready, I'm sure Clint will be happy to introduce you to more young people on the island."

She smiles. "That would be awesome." Her expression turns more solemn, and she purses her lips. "Maybe in a month or so. We still have to bury Mario. That is not something I ever expected to say, at least until we were older." She dabs the corners of her eyes with a tissue.

I pat her arm. "Be gentle with yourself, hon. There's no rush to do anything. Just take care of yourself and Georgie, and the rest will come when the time is right. Speaking of your cutie, where is he?"

"He's upstairs napping." She pulls a baby monitor with a screen out of her apron pocket to show me, Georgie snoozing in his crib.

Clutching my chest, I gush over the adorableness. "What a precious boy! I can't wait to give him a big hug when he gets up from his nap."

Coming out of my cuteness coma, panic overtakes me. Now's the time to talk to Lauren about her dad. Who knows if we'll be alone again? *This is so unnerving!* Hopefully, she doesn't notice the sweat dripping off my palms.

I plaster on the biggest smile I can manage. "So, you'd mentioned something about your dad coming to visit. Is he still planning a trip sometime soon?"

Her eyes widen. She starts to answer, but the sound of a tot crying comes from her apron. "I'm so sorry. He's teething, and I probably need to make a snack for him. Why don't you go sit on the veranda while Connie finishes setting up our lunch? I'll be down when he's settled again."

I try to hide my disappointment and nod. "Of course. Bring that lil' babe downstairs if he's feelin' up to it."

Lauren steps inside and goes upstairs. I walk through the living and dining rooms to the veranda, where Connie is pouring tall glasses of sweet tea. She looks up and grins.

"I'm so glad you came. We needed some company today. Where's Julia Caroline? I'd hoped to ask her opinion about something."

I look away and tuck a stray hair behind my ear. I've never been good at lying, especially to family and close friends. "I wasn't going to say anything because we don't know what's going on yet—she had a little fainting spell. She's at the hospital. They're keeping her for testing and to keep an eye on her."

Connie frowns. "Oh, my stars! I bet you're both so worried. Is she alright?"

My attempt to downplay the situation didn't take. What else can I tell her without sharing Julia Caroline's private business before she's ready?

I push back tears, and my lip trembles. "We don't have many answers yet. We're just praying and hoping for the best. That's all we can do. It's in God's hands."

Connie looks up. "I'm so sorry. We'll keep her in our prayers, too." She pauses. "And I understand what you mean about praying. I've been talking to God a lot lately. I'm glad his ears never get tired of listening to me rattle on nonstop. You don't realize how important that lifeline is until nothing else helps."

"Amen, sister. I'm glad we both have it."

"Me too. Please keep me posted on what the doctors say about Julia Caroline and if we can do anything for y'all."

I take her hands in mine. "We appreciate it."

We both tear up a little, and she embraces me.

"Julia Caroline is one tough cookie. If I had to guess, I'd wager Death is afraid of her, especially after all the ghosts she's sent over to the Other Side."

My jaw drops. "How do you know about all that ghostly business?" Julia Caroline and I have made it a point not to talk about spirits with our other friends ever since our former mayor banned the book she wrote on the topic back in the 70s. Connie is closer in age to our children, so she would have been little when all that happened.

She winks. "My mama is a seer. She kept a copy of Julia Caroline's book hidden in our attic, just in case some spirit got the bright idea to attach itself to our family. She made my sisters and me read it as we came of age, but luckily, I never needed to use what I read. I've never seen a haint. The blue paint on our porch ceiling probably helps, too."

I didn't know Connie's mama, Barbara, well. But some people in the Lowcountry believe that painting their porch ceiling light blue, the same color as the sky, keeps the haints from entering a house. If only it were that easy. A little bit of paint ain't gonna keep a determined spirit away from nothin'.

Should I tell Connie about Mario's visits?

As a mother, I would want to know. But I would be disturbed to learn that Wesley's spirit wasn't at rest and was being tormented by a malevolent ghost. While I think through how to handle the situation, Lauren and Georgie join us outside. The toddler's coos calm me.

CHAPTER 14

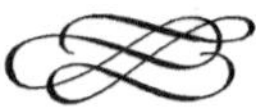

When we sit down to lunch, I try to lighten the mood and ask the ladies if they've taken Georgie to the beach yet. Lauren and Connie exchange a knowing look, and I have to ask what they're thinking about.

Oh, boy! It's like me to put my foot in my mouth. Looks like I've gone and done it again.

Lauren wrinkles her nose. "Umm, we went down to the beach yesterday, and a wave almost knocked Georgie down. Something really weird happened, though. It was like someone pushed him out of the water. It wasn't windy or anything like that. I could feel someone there with us. I can't explain it."

Connie sighs. "That's what I wanted to run by Julia Caroline … if she thought it might have been Mario trying to protect Georgie. Maybe it's wishful thinking that he's still with us. I miss my boy so much. I don't want to think he's trapped here, though. If he needs to move on, he should. I want him to be at peace."

Lauren closes her eyes and pulls Georgie close. My heart aches for them, but something stops me from spilling the tea right away.

I purse my lips. This is my chance to share, but once I let the cat out of the bag, there ain't no sending the kitty back. I reckon I don't have much of a choice. If I let them in on the secret, they might be able to help.

Connie grabs my shoulder. "You know something! Please tell us what is going on. I was up all night worrying, and I've got to get some sleep tonight."

I let out a deep exhale. "I'm so sorry y'all are going through this. It's so unfair. To answer your question, I've seen Mario's spirit more than once since he died. He can't control his whereabouts for some reason. I don't fully understand why. Julia Caroline hasn't seen anything like this either." I don't want to add to their pain by telling them about the malevolent spirit unless absolutely necessary.

Connie blows a kiss up toward Heaven. "Thank you, Jesus! I knew my boy was watching over little Georgie yesterday!"

Lauren's face turns as white as a sheet. "I've never believed in ghosts, but Mario's the first person in my family to die. I haven't ever had a reason to really think about hauntings or anything supernatural."

Wait! That means her father is alive and can't be the nasty devil who's tormenting Mario! Whew! I'm not as concerned about asking Lauren about a random person of interest in Mario's murder. This makes things a heck of a lot easier.

I rub my forehead and decide to run with it. "So, now that we're all on the same page, Mario mentioned y'all left California because of some man. Do you have any idea who he's talking about? Was it maybe someone he arrested, or did you have a neighbor who didn't like Mario? I can't imagine anyone not liking him … unless he threw them in jail, with good reason, of course. It got me thinking that person may be responsible for …"

Lauren's face falls. She starts to speak but bursts into tears and runs into the house with Georgie in her arms.

My heart breaks. That was the last thing I wanted to happen.

"Oh, dear. I'm so sorry, Connie. I really just want to help Mario, not hurt y'all."

A tear rolls down her cheek as she nods. "I know. We appreciate you. You understand better than anyone how hard it is to lose someone so young, especially when they're leaving a family behind. All you want for your children is for them to find happiness, and it's so very unfair that when they do, the bottom falls out. Things will never be the same for us."

"It's the absolute worst thing in the world. A parent should never have to bury their child. And a man shouldn't have to leave his family so soon, either. Y'all are in my prayers every single day."

"Thank you. We're so grateful to you and Julia Caroline for everything."

I hug her and offer to help clean up before I head back to the hospital. While we're putting away the leftovers, my thoughts about the killer stir again.

"Can you have Lauren call me when she's up to talking for a bit? If she could give me the names of anyone who might have wanted to harm Mario, I could tell him. It might be enough to put his mind at rest and let him cross over. He deserves to find peace."

Connie nods. "I'll let her have some space and try to give her a gentle nudge in a couple of days."

"Thank you. All of this is so difficult. I've been meaning to ask you—when are you planning Mario's service? Can I do anything to help you with arrangements?"

"We've decided not to have a funeral. Most of our family and Mario's friends don't live close by. Instead, we're going to have a quiet day of remembrance here tomorrow and watch old family movies together. The Chief wants to hold a memorial service for him next month. That will give everyone more time to travel."

I squeeze her hand. "That's understandable. Let me know if you need anything in the meantime."

After we finish cleaning up the dirty dishes, we say our goodbyes, and I drive back to the hospital. Life is always complex, but the past few days have been absolutely bonkers.

When Julia Caroline gets a clean bill of health, we're going on a good, long vacation, preferably a destination with no ghosts. Maybe sailing on a brand-new cruise ship would be a safe bet. It's a morbid thought, but no one should have died onboard yet. Hopefully, no hitchhiking spirits follow us. I can taste the piña coladas and strawberry daiquiris now.

I park the car and head inside. *Note to self—don't talk to spirits on the elevator this time.* I can't help but laugh. *So what if people think I'm nuts?*

A cold chill creeps down my spine, and I shrug it off. I'm not acknowledging any ghosties other than Mario today. I have enough drama on my plate without adding more chaos. The elevator doors slide open, and the malevolent spirit greets me. I pretend not to see the devil and walk straight through him.

"Hey! I know you can see me! I'm talking to you, Grandma! You're so old, you probably can't hear me. Maybe you can't see me either. I guess if I killed your best friend, it would take you a solid week to even notice she was gone."

I scream and spin around, ready to let that son of a biscuit eater have it, only to be face-to-face with Dr. Bow Tie instead. Heat rises up my face, and I wince. Why did it have to be him? What in all that is holy?

He straightens his glasses and clears his throat. "Ma'am, are you alright?"

How do I answer? Golly gee, Doc, an evil spirit murdered my grandson's partner and has decided to stalk me. My best friend is sick, and I'm barely hanging onto my sanity by the end of an unraveling thread. But yeah, everything is just lovely! Thank you kindly for asking! I reckon I shouldn't say those things, as much as I want to.

"Ma'am? Can I call someone for you?"

I smile. "Oh, no, Sugar. I'm just fine. It's been a long few days, but it's nothing I can't deal with."

He narrows his eyes at me. I guess I've earned that skepticism, but he doesn't know me or what I'm going through. People are so quick to judge each other. I don't understand. Mama always said to give other people grace, and I've tried my darnedest. I wish others would be just as considerate.

Since he's still staring, I wink. "Bless you for all the life-savin' work you do. Have a nice afternoon."

He nods and begins walking away from me. *How rude! Maybe I'm weird, but at least I have manners. Why on God's green earth am I wasting time thinking about this jerk?* I walk toward Julia Caroline's new room.

Stepping inside, I gawk. It's three times bigger than the small cave-like examination room in the ER, where she's been holed up for the past few days. This will be a lot more cozy for her, and there's actually an oversized sleeper chair where I can rest.

I sink down into the chair and put my feet up. *Oh, my goodness.* The tension in my back and shoulders melts, and I let out a deep exhale. I haven't relaxed like this in what seems like a century. Despite the chair being covered in the standard, sticky hospital vinyl material, it's much more comfortable than I expected. I'll just rest my eyes while Julia Caroline finishes her remaining tests. *Surely, she'll be back soon.*

Before I know it, I drift off, dreaming of sunny days on the beach with all my boys. A darkness looms just off the coast, and lightning strikes. *Hey, no fair! This is my dream, and I say no bad weather is allowed!*

If only I controlled my dreams.

CHAPTER 15

I wake to the sound of the hospital room door opening. It takes a moment for my eyes to adjust to the light filtering into the dark room. *How long was I out?*

The nurse pushes Julia Caroline's wheelchair into the room and helps her walk to the bed. *My best friend is completely capable of walking, so why is this nurse treating her like an invalid? It must be some lame hospital policy to prevent them from getting slapped with a lawsuit. At least I hope that's all.*

Julia Caroline crawls into bed and immediately turns away from me. *Excuse me?* I wait for the nurse to leave the room; then, I hop up from the recliner and crouch until I'm eye to eye with Julia Caroline. *I ain't gonna let her ignore me no matter how hard she tries.*

"Hey, hon, you were gone an awful long time. Is somethin' wrong?"

She tears up. "They found a couple of larger lumps during the MRI. The oncologist thought they're probably just fatty tissue deposits, but something is off. I'm not a doctor, but I've lived inside this body for sixty-seven years. I've tried to ignore how bad I've felt for the past few months, but I've been so tired and weak. I'd hoped to have at least another twenty years with my granddaughters. But if my time is up, the Good Lord will take me home."

I gasp. Julia Caroline isn't a Debbie Downer by nature. She always sees the light through the darkness and can find the silver lining on the bleakest day.

If she's feeling this way, I'll have to pick up the slack and help her stay positive. A few months ago, I read an article in the Ladies' Home Journal about a cancer survivor who swore that being optimistic saved her life. It sounds like I have my work cut out for me, but I'd do anything for this incredible lady.

"Look, babe—this is hard on both of us. Believe me, I wish our roles were reversed. I would gladly take your place any day of the week. No illness would stand a chance against your rays of sunshine. What would you do if I were the one lying in the hospital bed?"

Julia Caroline grunts. "I'd probably sing something like ... "

"Oh, I've got it!" I jump up and belt out, "Smile a while and give your face a rest. Point to the one you love the best. Shake hands with those nearby and greet them with a smile." We probably spent too many summers teaching vacation Bible school, but I've loved every moment of working with those kiddos alongside my best friend.

Someone knocks at the door, and Dr. Bow Tie steps inside. He gives me a smug smile. "Don't let me interrupt your concert."

My sassy mouth doesn't know when to stay shut. "Oh, that was just a little bit of Jesus coming straight from my lips. We all can use a dose of Him, wouldn't you say, Doc?" The lights in Julia Caroline's eyes are dancing, and her mouth twists awkwardly. I know she wants to laugh, but she has more self-control than I do.

He frowns. "I'm not here to have a religious debate. Let's sit down and talk."

I give him a thumbs up and plop down onto the recliner a little too hard. A noisy waft of air escapes as my leg rubs up against the squeaky vinyl on the seat cushion. *Well, that certainly sounded like I was passing gas. Thank goodness, I didn't!*

Julia Caroline's nostrils flare, and her cheeks puff out like she's holding her breath.

That's it! I can't hold back my laughter. And she can't either. We might be in our 60s, but our sense of humor hasn't matured since we were kids. Hearing her giggle does my heart so much good I don't give two hoots what grumpy ol' Dr. Bow Tie thinks. If this gave my bestie a bit of comedic relief during a stressful day, then so be it. He'll just have to be a grumpy old goat.

He clears his throat. "Ladies, let's get back on topic here. Tomorrow, I'll send a nurse to take Mrs. Mason to the lab for a couple of biopsies. Those will help us determine if the masses are benign or something worrisome. Do you have any questions for me?"

I nod. "When will we have the results?"

He cocks his head. "Should be within a few days."

Julia Caroline rubs her hands together anxiously. "If it turns out to be cancer, then what?"

"We try not to get ahead of ourselves here. You have no family history of breast cancer. Try not to worry yet. After we take our samples, you can go home and rest if you'd be more comfortable. No need for you or your sister to hang out here."

She thanks him, and he leaves the room. "I think he likes you so much he can't bear to be around you."

I snort. "Yeah, right. That man thinks I'm either drunker than Cooter Brown or nuttier than a five-pound fruitcake. He'll thank the good Lord the moment I leave the hospital. To be honest, I'm not his biggest fan either. I'd rather scrub the church's bathroom floors with a toothbrush than spend time with him."

"You're not gonna have a choice. He's my oncologist, supposedly the best in South Carolina, so if things go badly for me, you're going to be seeing a lot of him."

My eyes narrow. "It's a good thing you're going to be completely healthy, so I never have to be around this man ever again after you get your results."

Julia Caroline smiles. "Thank you for believing in me and not writing off my dreams for a healthy future. It would be so easy to give up, but we can't. Nothing like this is easy. But I'm lucky to have you as my best friend. It makes all the difference. But promise me you'll try to be nicer to my doctors?"

I scowl and wave my hand at her. "Okay. I'll try. It doesn't come naturally."

We both giggle. I'm thankful God saw fit to make us best friends.

I squeeze her hand, "Love ya, girl. I need some fresh air, but I'll be right back. Do you want anything from the gift shop or cafeteria?"

"Nope. Just going to rest a little. I may be asleep when you come back."

As I leave the room, her pale skin and un-toned arms catch my attention. It's odd. She's always kept a healthy glow and bulkier than average muscles from swimming laps every morning except late December through early March. The water is just too darn cold then.

When did she stop exercising and basking in the sunlight? For the difference to be so noticeable, it has to have been several months at least.

Why didn't I notice? I've been picking up shifts at the Sea Biscuit diner on the island for something to do and a little pocket money. I love my regular customers, but if Julia Caroline needs me, I'll step away from my job in a heartbeat and never look back.

The overwhelming aroma of pizza wafts out of the cafeteria, and my stomach rumbles. I really haven't been eating enough lately. I grab a couple of slices and a fountain drink. I sit down at a table and sip the soda. The effervescent bubbles tickle my nose. Dr. Bow Tie walks past me without saying a word. *What a rude man!*

I fake a cough and choke loudly. I can't help myself. I promised Julia Caroline I'd try being nicer, but he shouldn't snub me either. He turns back, looks my way, and his eyes dim.

Did I deserve that reaction? I've probably come off as a strange woman, but I haven't been cruel to him.

"Hey, Doc—why don't you join me?" I cover my mouth. *Ugh. Why did I say that?*

He shrugs. "Sure. Why not?"

I bite my tongue to hold back the insults that want to escape my mouth. He's Julia Caroline's doctor, and if the prognosis turns out to be bad, he could save her life. I need to play nice, no matter how hard it is. So, I grin until my cheeks ache.

He purses his lips. "You look like you're in pain."

"Oh, no, nothing like that. I'm just trying something different. It's taking some getting used to, but I'll be alright." That was a weird thing for me to say, but he doesn't flinch.

"Mrs. Mason seems like a lovely woman. Is she really your sister?" *Was that a personal attack?* I suck it up and ignore any cruel intent.

I sigh. I guess I've gotta come clean about that white lie. "Not by blood, but we've been best friends our whole lives. God knew what he was doing when he put us together."

He nods. "I'm still close to my dearest friend from elementary school. He saved my life once, and I'll always be in his debt." *Whoa ... Dr. Bow Tie has a heart.*

For the next hour, we reminisce about growing up in the Lowcountry and how things have changed over the years. It's funny—he's actually quite likable when he isn't judging me. Maybe he isn't half bad after all. I guess I should give him a chance, and not just because Julia Caroline asked.

CHAPTER 16

Just as I stand to go check on Julia Caroline, Lauren enters the hospital. Why is she here? Surely, most doctors' offices are closed by this hour. Something must be wrong—my stomach knots.

She looks over at me, waves, and starts walking toward us.

"Hey, hon. Are you alright?"

"Yeah. Connie asked me to call you, and I thought we should talk in person. I was hoping you hadn't left yet."

"Julia Caroline is having a biopsy tomorrow, so we'll be here at least another night." I gesture toward my dining companion. "Lauren, have you met Dr. Bow T-, I mean Dr. Bowman, yet? I don't guess you have, since you're new in town."

"No. I haven't. It's nice to meet you." Lauren shakes his hand. "I can come back later if you're in the middle of something."

Tom stands. "Oh, you don't need to go. I have to make my rounds before heading home to feed my dog his supper. It was nice meeting you. You can both call me Tom. Have a nice evening."

Before I say goodnight, I thank him for everything he's doing to take care of Julia Caroline.

"I'm happy to have her as a patient and you as a friend." He shivers. "It's been chillier than usual in the hospital. I keep telling the administrator to fix the AC or at least close the morgue door, so all the poor restless souls in there don't freeze us to death."

Was he joking? Surely ... I've never met a man with clair-voyant abilities, or at least none of them have admitted it. I give a half smile and wink at him.

As he walks away, something in me stirs, and heat rises up my face. Am I getting sick? That is the only explanation—I'm positive I don't have a crush on this bow-tie-wearing doofus. He's nice enough after he drops the judgmental act, but I don't need or want romance at my age.

Calm down, Nancy Parsons. It's not like he was flirting with you.

Lauren sits down at the table and smiles. "He's kinda cute if you're into the nerdy, bow tie type of guy. When are you going out with him again?"

I laugh. "This wasn't a date. We'd had some awkward exchanges, and Julia Caroline asked me to patch things up with him. Since he's her doctor, I'm trying to be nice and mature about everything, even though I'd rather paper cut my own eyeballs and feed them to the gators in the Intracoastal."

"If you say so. I saw the way he was looking at you. I think he was enjoying the view."

"Maybe I should paper cut his eyeballs so he can't look at me." After we both laugh, I shake my head. "Seriously, hon. I can't imagine dating anyone now, least of all him. Let's change the subject and chat about what's on your mind, though. I should check on Julia Caroline, and I'm sure you want to get home to Georgie."

Lauren draws a deep breath. "Sorry. I guess I was stalling because I'm dreading talking about why we left California. But if it can help Mario find peace, I'll do whatever it takes."

"I hate you're having to think about such painful things, but I want to figure out who this person is."

She coughs and turns slightly purple, green, and finally, pale. *Oh, no! This girl is going to throw up!* The only thing I despise more than hospitals and hitchhiking ghosts is vomit. It's the most disgusting bodily fluid known to man. Just the thought of it makes me nauseous.

"Hon, you look like you're about to be sick."

"I'll be okay… well, I will be … I think." She pauses and sighs. "Here goes—when I was in high school, I fell in love with the gorgeous quarterback of the football team. It's such a cliché. He didn't have a clue who I was until I fainted right in front of his locker. What are the odds? He called 911 and even rode in the ambulance with me. After we dated for a month, he promised he would always watch out for me and said I belonged to him. I was too naive to comprehend the extent of his possessiveness at the time."

I shiver. "Narcissists have a way of preying on women. I'm guessing you broke up with him, and he wasn't happy."

"Yeah. He threatened to kill me and himself when I left for college, saying he didn't trust me not to cheat. I ended things immediately and got a restraining order. He seemed to disappear for a few years, but when I started dating Mario my senior year, he crept out of the woodwork."

Not surprising. It must be written in the Narcissist 101 Handbook—find a pretty woman and convince her you are the be-all-end-all for her. If she isn't smart enough to realize your awesomeness, stalk her until she realizes you're her dream come true or worst nightmare. Either way, you have your girl exactly where you want her—you're all she can think about.

"So he's been harassing y'all for the past five years, give or take?"

Lauren gulps hard and nods. "He's everywhere we go. Six months ago, he showed up at our house and threatened to kill all of us." A tear rolls down her cheek. "Mario took out a new restraining order, but I've been terrified ever since."

Oh, my Lord! My blood is boiling, and I'm beside myself. I could absolutely choke anyone who pulls nasty tricks like this to scare people and get their way. I don't want to make Lauren relive the gory details, so I'd better make my point.

I take Lauren's hand. "I'm so sorry you've been through all this. Can you tell me his name?"

Her nostrils flare. "Dan Sutton."

Cheese and rice! Was Mario's cryptic note referring to D-A-N, not D-A-D? Calm down so you don't frighten this poor child!

"Thank you, hon. That's what I needed to know. Can I buy you a cup of coffee or a donut? Neither are as good as home-made, but for store-bought, they ain't half bad."

She shakes her head. "Thanks, but I should probably head back to Connie's house to check on Georgie. He loves being with her, but he might be afraid if I'm not around when he wakes up. Let us know when Julia Caroline gets to go home. We'll come to visit her. Georgie has been drawing pictures for her."

"Sounds like a deal. We'd love to see y'all, and Julia Caroline will be tickled pink to have a Georgie original masterpiece."

We say our goodbyes, and I stay in the cafeteria to process our conversation. Dan's last name, Sutton, sounds so familiar. It's a common name in these parts for sure, but I feel like there's more to it than that. But I shrug off the thought and call Clint. When he answers, I tell him what Lauren shared with me.

He goes silent for a few seconds. Did our call get disconnected?

"Hon, are you still there?"

Clint sighs. "Yup. Just trying to decide what in the heck to do next. I'm going to check our database to find out if he's been arrested recently. If he's a repeat offender in Los Angeles, we could ask the LAPD to bring him in for questioning for another crime. Hang tight for just a sec."

My grandson is a genius!

"Hey, that is a great idea. I'm gonna go up and check on Julia Caroline. Can I call you back in a little while?"

"Cool. I haven't found anything yet. I'll text you if I do."

After we hang up, I step onto the elevator. This is usually where the nonsense with the devil himself goes down. I'm not in the mood to entertain him, but maybe I can ask about his connection to Dan. They have to be working together. Can Dan communicate with the dead? He must have the gift. I don't want to ask Lauren. As weirded out as she was about Mario hanging around, she doesn't need to know about this unidentified pain in the rear spirit. Since she can't communicate with him, what good would it do?

The elevator stops on the first floor, but the doors don't open. Instead, a silver fog sparkles in the corner. I roll my eyes. *Great ... I guess we're doing this again.* I tap my foot, waiting for him to make his grand entrance.

I yawn. "Sugar, this is becoming so dang predictable. I ain't gettin' any younger. Let's get it over with. C'mon already."

His apparition finally solidifies, at least as much as any ghost does.

"Sounds like you're glad to see me, Grandma. I'm not surprised. Everyone loves seeing Dan the Man! Well, here I am!"

My jaw drops. This is Dan? I didn't think Mario's murderer was dead himself. How did he shoot a gun? I've seen ghosts do some horrific things, but they usually lack the fine motor skills required to pull a trigger. As I read the name on his baseball cap —Sutton Construction, serving the Southeast since 1984.

I should have guessed—*Dan is related to those Suttons!* They built a hotel on Sweetgrass Island in the 80s and let it burn down, with several of their employees and guests inside. I swanee, I ain't heard a sadder story in my life. The Suttons should have gone to prison for negligence or at least been ashamed. But they came out of it looking like a shiny penny. Of course, they have a narcissistic younger relation ... son ...

nephew … whatever this devil is to them. At least I understand who I'm dealing with.

What's mystifying is that Lauren didn't seem to know Dan was dead. How can that be? It has to be a recent development.

"Cat got your tongue, Grandma?" He sneers, and I want to slap that stupid expression off his face.

"Oh, not at all. I'm just wondering how a ghost shot a police officer on a busy interstate in broad daylight without more people noticing a gun hovering around by itself. Seems like that sort of thing would draw attention."

He scowls. "Not that it's any of your business, but I wasn't dead yet."

I put my hands on my hips. "Lordy, what took the magnificent Dan Sutton down? It had to be something like a knife fight in a bar or an undiagnosed heart condition." I tap my upper lip with my index finger. "On second thought, maybe a little girl pushed you into traffic. Smart kid. I'll have to find her and give her a high five."

His cheeks redden, and steam encircles his face. "I was on my way to pay Lauren a visit after Mario died, and some moron in a semi-truck ran me off a bridge. I drowned." He growls.

I slap my cheek playfully. "Oh, dear. Did I hit a nerve?"

"Shut up, Grandma!" He puffs out his chest and looks down at me.

"Nope. I'm not done talking yet. Why are you keeping Mario from appearing to us? My guess is you don't want him to communicate with Lauren because you still want to control her from beyond the grave. Once a narcissist, always a narcissist. Since I've got you figured out, you may as well scoot on around to the Other Side."

We couldn't get that lucky, but I'm done messing around with this fool. I pull out my cross pendant and the small Bible I keep in my purse. I flip to James 4:7 and begin reading, *"Submit yourselves therefore to God. Resist the devil, and he will flee from you."*

Dan's brow furrows as I hold out the cross and scream, "Be gone, devil. In Jesus' name. Amen!"

I hold my breath as his crumpled face fades into his trademark iridescent vapor. *Whew!* I've gotta find a more permanent fix for banishing this idiot, but this works for now. I need to support Julia Caroline without worrying about little old him.

CHAPTER 17

When I enter Julia Caroline's dark room, she shields her eyes from the hallway light.

"I was one minute from sending out a search party to hunt you down. Where've ya been?"

I tell her about everything Lauren shared and my run-in with Dan. "I'm so dang frustrated, but at least we know who murdered Mario now. I reckon I should tell Clint about Dan, so he can stop looking for suspects. But it's not fair that Dan won't pay for the crime he committed. Death was too good for this hoodlum. We've at least gotta send him to the Other Side so he can't harass Mario anymore."

"How are you going to manage that from the hospital? Do they happen to have a blue bottle tree in the courtyard? You could use a bottling spell to trap that jerk inside a bottle and throw it into the marsh for an alligator to swallow."

Some people in the Lowcountry keep bottle trees with a dozen or more bottles in their yards to capture evil spirits. I haven't tried using one yet, but it's definitely worth looking into.

I chuckle. "I knew you'd have some creative ideas. I've been using my cross pendant and Bible to send him away, but it never lasts for long. We need something good and lasting."

Julia Caroline sits up straight. "I've got it—we can convince someone to get his face tattooed on their butt and trap him there! It doesn't get more permanent or perfect than that."

I laugh. "But who wants the devil tattooed on their hind-end?"

"Uh—I've seen more scandalous ink every day on the beach, especially during spring break. By the time those partying college kids have drunk their third round of cheap, rancid tequila shots for breakfast, I'd say they'd tattoo just about anything you can imagine on any unmentionable body part. Of course, nowadays, people are getting rid of tattoos they don't like anymore."

"You're too much!" I giggle at the mental image of depraved young things walking around with red and black cartoon devils inked on their skinny bottoms, barely covered by what passes for a decent bathing suit. They weren't raised right, and it shows.

My ribs ache from all the laughter, and I couldn't be happier about the throbbing pain. Who would have thought that would be possible? This is the reason my best friend has to live forever. Anytime I'm depressed, she pulls me back up out of the bottomless pits of despair and makes me forget all my problems.

It's not fair that her health conundrum is the battle we're fighting now, instead of something we can control. We've kicked so many horrific, malevolent spirits' booties. I wish this was just as easy.

I can't tell her how much I'm hurting. She needs me to be the strong one. So, I keep this between God and me. *Surely, it isn't her time just yet. Lord—I beg you!* Does God get tired of me sounding like a darn broken record? I hope not, because I'll never stop praying for Julia Caroline.

Julia Caroline gasps, and I turn around to find out what caused the sudden reaction.

"What's wrong?"

She pants and clutches her chest. "I'm having a shooting pain in my breast."

I jump up and press the nurse call button. They'd better hurry. She hasn't asked for a single thing yet or given them a lick of trouble. I'm the nuisance in our duo, and I'm more than fine with that. Julia Caroline closes her eyes. It would be great for her to rest, but I can tell she is hurting too much to fall asleep. I rummage through my purse. I wish I had something to relieve her pain, but I don't have so much as an aspirin with me.

What is taking them so long? I'm sure they're beyond busy, but she needs help now.

I'm tempted to go to the nurses' station and give them a piece of my mind. But I remember my promise to be nice. It doesn't come naturally to me when someone I love is suffering.

Being helpless isn't my strong suit either. I try to block out my instincts to go feral on the nurses.

A few minutes later, a nurse comes into the room and asks Julia Caroline a battery of questions. She promises to return with medication shortly. *It's about dang time, for goodness' sake!*

My best friend looks so frail and old lying on the hospital bed. I want to scream, so I cover my mouth with my hand and make myself focus on something else. The first thing that pops into my head is planning a visit with my boys. It's been way too long since we were all together. We need to make it a priority as soon as this lovely lady is back home, safe and sound.

Clint texts me to say he's stopping by. I sink down in the chair, and my shoulders relax a little. The only silver lining to all this crap is that at least I don't have to worry about him chasing after Dan to avenge Mario's death.

Thank God for small favors!

The nurse finally returns with some painkillers and a pitcher of ice water. Julia Caroline opens her eyes and takes the medication.

After the nurse leaves the room, Julia Caroline closes her

eyes again. I hope the meds help her rest, but I can't just sit here and stare at the ceiling. I write a note, saying I'll be back shortly, and place it on the bedside table. Hopefully, taking a walk will clear my mind.

I step outside her room and start walking toward the elevator.

"Hello, Grandma. Looking for trouble?" I pivot and stick my finger out, ready to give Dan a piece of my mind. In his place stands Clint.

Dropping my hands to my waist, I gasp. "Since when have you called me Grandma? That's not okay! I'm "Gram' to you!"

Clint raises his eyebrows. "What are you talking about? I didn't say anything."

Dang it all! Dan must have been here, but where did he go? I don't need this right now. "Oh, boy, have I got a lot to tell you." I grab Clint's hand and take him to the garden, where I tell him everything.

He shakes his head. "I'll never get used to all this crazy ghost business. I'm gonna follow up and make sure this Dan guy's unlikely story checks out. It sounds a little fishy, but I guess anything can happen. How did he die anyway?"

"Something about a semi-truck running him off a bridge. He didn't tell me the nitty-gritty details of exactly how or where it went down."

Clint makes a fist and punches his other hand. "This beats all. Doesn't it?" He doesn't wait for an answer. "I can't believe some deranged idiot had the nerve to kill Mario and die before he served his time. Gah—I don't know what to think, but at least there's one less murderer on the streets." He wipes his eye—was that a tear? My heart is breaking. I haven't seen him cry since he was a kid.

"I'm so sorry. It kills me to see you and Connie's family hurtin' like this. I wish I could rewind time and warn Mario."

"There's nothing we can do about that now."

I stomp my foot, scattering a pile of clumped mulch under

my feet. "But we'll make sure that the son of a biscuit eater goes to the Other Side so he can't torment anyone ever again. I don't need this crap with everything that's going on with Julia Caroline."

"How is she? Have the doctors told y'all anything new yet?"

I frown. "Not really. If something horrible happens to her …. what will I do?"

Clint grabs my trembling hand and squeezes it. "You know as well as I do that she's a tough cookie. I don't think you need to worry. I'll keep her in my prayers all the same. That never hurts."

"Thank you, hon. It doesn't hurt at all. Why don't you head home and rest? You've had a long day, too."

"Are you sure? I hate to leave you here alone."

I nod. There's no point in keeping him here when he can't do anything to help. One Parsons family member spending the night at the hospital, worrying about Julia Caroline, is quite enough.

He sighs. "Well, I can always come back. Just send me a text, and I'll be right here."

"I hope when I call you tomorrow, I'll get to say we're heading home. I'd give anything to sleep in my own bed, knowing that Julia Caroline is as fit as a fiddle. That would be a huge relief. That's an understatement, but you know what I mean."

"I'll be praying for both of y'all. And I'm gonna look into what happened to Dan. I hate to share more bad news with Lauren, but hopefully, it will be a relief to know her stalker is dead."

"Let me know what you find out."

"Will do, but Gram—be careful around this ghost. I don't get how any of this works, and I don't really want to become an expert. But if he's half as dangerous as he was before he died … I don't like the idea of you being alone with him."

My heart warms at the sentiment behind Clint's words. He wraps me in a bear hug, and we say goodbye.

After he leaves, I go back inside the hospital and return to Julia Caroline's room to find her fast asleep. My shoulders relax at the sight of my best friend curled up on her side. She looks more like herself again, not the fragile aging woman I saw lying there earlier.

Maybe everything will be alright after all. I settle into the recliner and drift off to sleep.

CHAPTER 18

The sound of hushed voices whispering wakes me up. Two nurses stand beside Julia Caroline's bed, hooking up new IV bags and adjusting wires. My best friend's eyes are wide as they continue fussing with the machinery.

I stretch and yawn. "What's going on?"

Julia Caroline frowns. "They're getting ready to take me back for the biopsy." She pauses and hugs herself. "Dr. Bowman stopped by. If they find something during the biopsy, they're going to remove the largest lumps right then. I asked them to call you either way. If it's bad, let Susan know."

I shudder at the thought of calling Julia Caroline's daughter, Susan, with bad news.

Shaking my head, I pat her hand. "It's gonna be okay. Don't you worry about a thing. Just focus on staying calm. I'll be right here when you get back."

A nurse lowers the head of Julia Caroline's bed while the other pulls the blankets over her body and tucks them underneath the mattress.

I lean over and hug my best friend before they wheel her out of the room. "I love you, Julia Caroline Mason. You'll see ...

we're going to get you all fixed up and back home later today. I'll make us a mess of shrimp and rice and some apple pie and ice cream for dessert."

My heart pounds furiously. *Should I be worried about that? Nah —at least I'm at the hospital if I go into cardiac arrest.* I shiver and yawn. I'm exhausted, but there's no way I'm going back to sleep now. I can't just sit here while I wait for Julia Caroline to get out of surgery. So, what should I do? I didn't stop by the gift shop yesterday. I need some toiletries. Brushing my teeth and hair would probably help me feel a little less haggard.

I leave a note with my cell phone number on the dry-erase board hanging by the door and wander down the dimly lit hallway.

When I finally make it to the gift shop, I zone out while looking through magazines and books. None of the words on the covers makes sense. I guess I'd better stick to shopping for the necessities. Otherwise, I might unknowingly buy a magazine for gator wrestlers. Instead, I pick out a simple, clear toiletry bag filled with travel-sized basics. That should do the trick. I pay the cashier and head back toward the elevator.

I look down at my watch but don't stop walking, almost bumping into someone. I look up to see Dr. Bow Tie ... er ... Tom.

His brow furrows. "I was looking for you. It's Mrs. Mason. Can we talk for a moment?" I gulp. *My heart is going to shatter into a million pieces right here and now.* He leads me to a far corner of the cafeteria, away from people trying to eat their lunches. I don't know this man. I can't cry and definitely don't want to turn into a blubbering idiot in front of him. So, how do I respond to the bad news he's about to deliver? I force myself to empty my mind. I'll have to wait to process whatever he says.

We sit down at a table for two. This isn't the second date Lauren had in mind for us. I can't make eye contact with him, or I will lose it.

"Are you alright, Ms. Parsons?"

I wipe a bead of sweat from my brow. "I'm not sure yet. Can you tell me what's going on with Julia Caroline first? Then, I'll let you know."

He sighs. "I hate to have to tell you this, but the biopsy came back positive for cancerous cells. We're preparing her for surgery now. I don't believe in letting these things go, especially when the patient has felt unwell for some time. Mrs. Mason is unsure exactly when the fatigue set in, but she knows it's been at least six or seven months. Does that sound right to you?"

A tear rolls down my cheek. "She never complained to me. I didn't realize anything was wrong until last week. She tried to keep it a secret, but I found out about her doctor appointments and invited myself to tag along."

"I'm so sorry. We're going to remove these masses tonight. Hopefully, we'll get clear margins, and she'll be in good shape afterward. Even if that is the case, we may still do some radiation or a low dose of chemo. I'd rather be overly cautious than to make someone go through this twice if I can avoid it."

My throat tightens, so I just nod. I want this to be the end of the nightmare for both of us. We've been through so many tough moments, but nothing has prepared us for this.

He furrows his brows. "Are you going to be okay? I need to get back to the operating room. The nurses are getting her prepped, but I can ask the chaplain to come sit with you if you want."

"No, thank you. Please go fix her up. I'll ask my grandson to stay with me while we wait. I need to call Julia Caroline's daughter in case she wants to head this way from Knoxville. How long will the surgery take?"

"Probably about an hour, plus an hour or so in recovery. I'll call you personally when we finish, so I can give you a full report of what I find. Unfortunately, we have to send this off for testing. I won't have the lab results for at least a few days."

I thank him, and when he walks away, I lay my head down on the ice-cold table. *This can't be happening!* I make myself breathe in, count to five, and exhale, count to five, and repeat the process until my heart rate slows somewhat. *What am I gonna do? I have to be Julia Caroline's rock no matter what. Get your crapola together, Nancy Parsons!*

My hands tremble as I text Clint to update him, but that's easy peasy compared to what I have to do next.

I clear my throat and force back tears that threaten to spill down my cheeks as I dial Susan's number. She's probably at her boutique. The shop is just starting to get busy, so she's been working crazy long hours. *Please pick up, Susan!*

"Hey, Nan! What's going on? I was just thinking we hadn't chatted this week."

I sigh. I should have made Julia Caroline call Susan before we got to this point. Out of her four kids, Susan has stayed the closest over the years, calling and visiting as often as possible. I consider her and her daughters my family, too, and they hold a special place in my heart. All the same, it's simply not right that she's having to hear the horrible news from me instead of her mother.

I swallow hard. "Hon, this is tough to talk about, so I'm going to just spit it out. Your mom is sick. We don't know how bad it is yet. She's in surgery right now."

I continue sharing everything I know so far, but I don't allow myself to think too deeply about the words I'm saying. When I finish, she doesn't respond. *Did we get disconnected?*

Drawing a deep breath, I massage my temples. "Are you still there?"

Susan coughs. "Sorry. This is just a shock. I had no idea she was feeling bad. We talked a couple of days ago. Why didn't she mention it to me then?"

I wipe the corner of my eye. "I don't know, hon. I wish she had."

Susan grows quiet again, and I sit quietly for a moment to let her absorb everything. *Heaven knows she is scared. What should I say?*

Thankfully, she finds her words first.

"Sorry—I'm struggling to wrap my head around all this craziness, but I'm grateful you're with her. I need to go home, pack a bag, and take care of a few things. I'll be on the road before lunchtime. Please call me when she's out of surgery or if the doctor talks to you. And, Nan?"

"Yes, hon?"

"I love you. Thank you for taking care of Mom."

"Of course. I love you, too." I can't squeak out another word, so I hang up. I can't hold back the tears any longer. I cry for my best friend, her family, and myself. None of us deserves to be going through this disaster. Once the floodgates open, there's no closing them for a bit. This is one of those times when I've bottled up my emotions too long, and they overflow until I've cried out every last tear.

At least the hospital cafeteria is mostly empty, so I don't have an audience for my pity party. If I could banish cancer to the Other Side, I would tell it to kiss my grits.

Speaking of sending villains where they belong, it's bewildering that Dan hasn't been around for several hours, not that I'm complaining. I dry my eyes and grunt.

What is it going to take to send him away for good?

Usually, Julia Caroline says we need a major life event to help send a malevolent spirit to their final resting place. But none of my friends or family members are getting married or having a baby anytime soon. I refuse to entertain the idea of anyone dying. Of course, there are exceptions to this necessity. Back in the 1990s, which seems like a lifetime ago, we used my mother's prayer box charm bracelet to give the spirit of my ex-husband, Carl, a one-way ticket to his final destination. Messages magically materialized inside the box-shaped charm and guided us through each step we needed to take.

Unfortunately, I don't have the bracelet or its amazing connection to the Other Side. There has to be another way.

CHAPTER 19

*D*eep in thought, I jump when my cell phone vibrates on the table. I scowl. I can face the most malevolent, ornery spirits in the world without flinching, but a little old phone can scare the pants off me. I pick it up and read a text from Susan, saying her daughters, aka Julia Caroline's prized granddaughters, are already on their way. The three girls had been working as camp counselors in Asheville and left for South Carolina shortly after their mom called.

My heart flip-flops at the thought of seeing these angels. I love them like my own. I've never had a daughter or granddaughter, so over the years, I've made it my sole purpose when they're around to spoil them rotten. They make it easy.

Julia Caroline is going to throw a hissy fit when she finds out so many of her relatives are coming to fuss over her.

Ugh ... I just need her to be out of surgery. Once I'm positive she's okay, then I'll dump this news on her. I leave the room to buy a soda and a pack of peanut butter crackers from the cafeteria vending machines. Maybe I should run out and pick up a tasty, comforting lunch for us. Who could stay mad with a plate of fried seafood and a buttermilk biscuit sitting on their bedside table?

As I start walking toward my car, my phone rings. I look down at the caller ID to see it's a call from within the hospital. I gulp hard and answer. Sure enough, it's Tom on the other line with an update.

"I want to be upfront with you, we're not positive we got clear margins. Her situation was more complex than expected. We're sending the samples to pathology, and no matter the results, we're going to keep a close eye on everything for a good long while. Why don't you come up to her room in about ten minutes? I'll talk to both of you some more there."

Instead of freaking out, I thank him and hang up. But my stomach feels like I've swallowed a yo-yo. All this surgery did was muddy the waters even more until we get the pathology results.

Back to plan B for lunch. I guess I'll grab those vending machine crackers and a soda after all. Maybe Clint can pick up some real grub for our dinner. I don't want to keep Julia Caroline or Tom waiting. Besides, I may as well warn her about the impending family reunion, so she can kick and scream and calm down before her girls arrive. *Is it my fault everyone loves her more than life itself?* She'll be glad to see all her girls once she gets over the initial surprise.

I step onto the elevator, and the door refuses to close. *What on earth? Please don't let Dan mess with me—I'm out of patience for his antics.*

Slapping the close-door button again, the door finally shuts. *What a relief!* I try to mentally prepare for my conversation with Julia Caroline, reminding myself that this has been an even harder day for her.

An iridescent bubble materializes, and I groan. I'm in no mood for Dan.

As the bubble transforms into a figure, Mario's face appears, and I reach out and hug him. "It's so good to see you, hon! How did you sneak past Dan?"

Mario shrugs. "There's no rhyme or reason for it as far as I can tell, but he's been missing for several hours. I waited to make sure he wasn't just going to come back and wail on me. I wish I understood more about how all this works. But I'm here now. Can you help me get rid of him permanently? I don't think I'll be able to cross over until he can't mess with Lauren, Georgie, or my mom."

I nod. "I've sent him off for short periods of time. I want to find a more permanent fix. Do you remember Julia Caroline, my best friend? She just found out she has cancer. She's waiting for me in her room."

"Oh, no! Clint dated her granddaughter, right?"

"Yeah. He and Blake dated throughout high school."

"I hope she is okay."

"Thanks, hon. I promise the first free second I have, I'm going to dream up a way to send this loser away for good."

"Thank you." He pauses. "I can't believe he killed me and then turned around and died himself. That is pretty dumb timing on his part. And it's definitely a case of karma coming back around for someone."

"He's a classic narcissist and didn't think the rules applied to him. What could possibly kill someone who is above everyone and everything else? Well, he found out … didn't he? I hate that means he's been able to cause you more chaos when you're trying to transition to your final destination. If anyone ever deserved to be in Heaven, it's you, along with my Wesley and his wife, MaryAnne. I hope you'll look them up when you make it there."

He grins. "It's a deal. Prayers for Julia Caroline. I'll check in as soon as I can."

The elevator door opens, still stuck on the main floor. *Dang —let's try this again.* I push the button for Julia Caroline's floor, and the darn contraption finally goes up as expected. Why do ghosts love finding me on the elevator? I reckon they know I'm a captive audience, seeing how I'm confined inside.

When I enter Julia Caroline's room, Tom is standing beside her bed. She is pale, and the aftereffects of the anesthesia are apparent in her eyes.

Tom turns to me. "I was just sharing Mrs. Mason's prognosis with her. Unfortunately, it's a waiting game with the lab. You can expect to take her home tomorrow, and we'll set up some outpatient visits for next week to go over the results in detail."

"I'm glad she can go home to recover. Thanks so much for everything you're doing."

"My pleasure. I'm going to let you two catch up." He smiles. "Oh, before I go—Ms. Parsons, please tell me if I'm being too forward, but would you like to grab coffee somewhere outside of the hospital sometime?"

Julia Caroline winks at me, and I blush. "Yes. I'd love to. You can call me Nancy or Nan—that's what most of my friends call me."

He smiles. "It's a date, Nan. I'll talk to you ladies later."

After he closes the door, Julia Caroline fans herself with the plastic cover from her plate. "I do declare, it's getting mighty hot in here. Maybe it's the drugs they gave me, but it seems like there's some seriously swoon-worthy chemistry taking place between y'all."

I giggle and throw the edge of the white flannel blanket from the hospital bed up toward her face. "Hush your mouth, cow!"

She throws her hands up. "Hey, now … I'm the patient. You have to be gentle with me, remember?"

I roll my eyes. "You're as delicate as a freight train. Well, you might be as steamed as one after you hear the news I need to share. Just remember you told me to call Susan if things took a more serious turn."

Julia Caroline cringes as I share the events precipitating from my chat with Susan, but she waves her hand. "It's okay. I can't wait to see my precious girls. I hate that they left their jobs, but some gossip and girl time may be just what the doctor ordered. Speaking of doctors … I'm so excited for you and Dr. Bowman. Dr. and Mrs. Bowman … I like the sound of that."

"It's just a casual coffee date. We're not eloping or planning a June wedding. I'm still not sure I even like him as a friend."

"Not yet. Give it a little more time. We'll see where this goes with the good doctor."

"You're incorrigible." But I have to admit, I started wondering what might happen between Tom and me. Will our first date be our last, or do we have the makings for an actual relationship?

I haven't had much of a dating life since Brian left town to help his daughter, and I've been perfectly content with my life as Gram to my incredible grandsons and Julia Caroline's lovely granddaughters. They keep me young and on my feet, as I live vicariously through all their adventures.

Still, who am I to say no if God sends a doctor to be my companion? It would be nice to have a standing dinner date every Saturday evening and someone to sit with at church on Sunday. I don't need more than that from a man. I already have my best friend, and I'm not looking to replace her anytime soon, especially with a husband.

Before I forget, I share my conversation with Mario with Julia Caroline. "What do you think I should do? There is no life event taking place. I don't have another magical family heirloom for us to use to send him away."

Julia Caroline rubs her chin. "No, but I might. Remind me when we go home to look for my grandmother's pearls. My family has used them to get rid of especially problematic spirits for decades. I think they might do the trick. I'll explain later."

"No! You love that necklace. I don't wanna risk losing or breaking the strand while we're doing God knows what to get rid of this jerk. You know how unpredictable things can be."

She waves her hand. "Yeah … I understand why you're worried, but I don't foresee anything happening to them. It's not like he can take them with him. We can always have the pearls restrung if the ribbon breaks. That's the worst that is likely to happen."

"I hope you're right. We'll cross that bridge when we get there."

Julia Caroline stretches and yawns, and I tell her she needs to take a nap before her whole crew shows up. The scowl on her face is overpowered by another even bigger yawn. She mutters something about closing her eyes for a few minutes, and seconds later, she's lost the fight with the sandman.

When she starts snoring louder than an out of breath wild boar running uphill, I have to hold back a laugh. If her snoring cadence is any indication, she's going to be out for a while.

CHAPTER 20

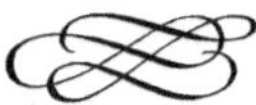

After strolling through the hospital's gift shop and cafeteria to buy some more snacks, I wander back toward Julia Caroline's room. As I turn the last corner before the elevator bank, I see three familiar faces—Julia Caroline's beautiful granddaughters, Blake, Brittany, and Elaina. I open my arms wide to embrace each of them. We sit down in the lobby to catch up for a few minutes.

Blake, the eldest sister, gulps. "How is Granny Mason?"

I don't want to scare them more than they already are. "Your granny is just as feisty as ever. Even if this turns out to be cancer, she's going to kick it right in the teeth and send it packin' before breakfast."

Brittany, the youngest, giggles. "Sounds like Granny Mason, alright." She is deaf but reads lips well and speaks vocally so clearly that I sometimes forget she can't hear. My mother's sister was profoundly deaf and didn't have the education to equip her for communicating with most hearing people. American Sign Language was her only choice, and it was up to my grandmother to ensure she learned ASL.

Thankfully, my family all learned to sign, something I

consider a huge blessing. I was so glad to see the communication options Brittany had available as she developed language skills as a toddler and throughout school. She's such a brilliant young woman, just like her sisters.

Elaina, in true middle child form, doesn't say much ... yet. Ever the inquisitive one, I'm sure she will have some complicated questions for the doctors later.

I take them up to Julia Caroline's room, and we tiptoe inside. My best friend is still fast asleep. The three girls sit together on the pullout sleeper chair, where I've been resting, and I plop down on the smaller, wobbly armchair. This furniture leaves a lot to be desired, but it's what we have. It's not like we're staying at the Charleston Place Hotel, one of the finest hotels in the area.

Brittany signs in ASL, "Umm .. she looks like she is in pain. Why does she have to suffer so much? Can't they give her some meds?" The other girls and I all lock our gaze on their grandmother. Julia Caroline furrows her brow and murmurs something in her sleep. My heart sinks at the sight of her pinched facial expression.

Elaina wipes a tear from her eye, and I have to look away. *This is the worst!*

As hard as it is for me to see my best friend suffering this way, these youngsters have always idolized their incredible Granny Mason. They must be hurting something dreadful right now. There isn't much I can say that I haven't already shared with them, but I need to lift their spirits somehow.

A nurse enters the room and checks the IV machine. Julia Caroline stirs, and I want to scream at the nurse for the disruption. They're pumping saline into her veins. Sleep is more important for her well-being than anything that stupid contraption is doing. Surely, it could have waited. Julia Caroline's eyes flutter rapidly again.

Is she awake? I'm not happy about the abrupt interruption, but if she woke up, did she see that she has company ... her most favorite guests of all time?

Blake stands and walks closer to the hospital bed as if she is examining her grandmother. Julia Caroline shoots straight up in bed and wraps her arms around Blake's neck, nearly pulling Blake down onto her lap. I snort—*what incredible comedic timing!* This lady is a nut, and I mean that in the best way possible. It's a miracle she hasn't lost her zany sense of humor during all the chaos. Both women are laughing so hard that they're on the brink of crying.

Thank goodness Julia Caroline helped lighten the mood. Now, I don't have to create a lame distraction for the girls to take their minds off their grandmother's condition.

Each of Julia Caroline's granddaughters takes a turn hugging her and asking a couple of questions. When they seem satisfied with her answers, they excuse themselves for a few minutes and leave the room. I know they're overwhelmed and probably tired from their trip, but they're young and they will bounce back quickly. At their age, it's nothing some hot coffee can't fix.

After they've been gone for a little bit, Julia Caroline turns to me. "Is Susan here yet?"

"She had to finish up some stuff at her shop and pack, but she should be here soon."

Julia Caroline sighs. "I'm relieved the girls got here before her. I couldn't deal with that much sadness at one time. They were radiating doom and gloom from their pores. It was a lot to bear. I had to break up their bad energy, so I didn't get upset again, either. I didn't want them to see me cry. We would have been the hot mess express."

She's right. As hard as this has been on all of us, we all need to keep the mood as light as possible. Julia Caroline deserves that much consideration from all of us. I texted Susan to ask her to meet me in the lobby when she arrives so we can chat.

What a day! This week feels like it's lasted an entire year!

I'm not letting Julia Caroline wallow either. I grab both of her hands. "C'mon, stand up! We're gonna take a walk."

She doesn't move. "No. I should stay in case the girls come back or a nurse stops by."

"Nah … I'll text your girls, and we can stop by the nurses' station to let them know you need some fresh air. It'll do you good to get out of this room. And I need a walk, too."

I fire off a text to Susan and the girls, asking them to let us know when they're ready to meet up again. There's no reason they can't join us for our stroll instead of all of us sitting in a depressing hospital room, thinking about the worst outcomes for Julia Caroline. Really, they should have discharged her today, but I'm sure there's some legal reason they can't. I've never cared to understand insurance companies and hospital policies. *Phooey to that load of horse manure.*

Julia Caroline grumbles as she shimmies out of bed and stands. I want to tell her to stop acting like a child, but I stop myself. This is a horrible time in her life. She'll be happier once she's out and about. No need to hurt feelings and make things more difficult.

We open the door and walk toward the nurses' station. Three women, who appear to be in their 30s and 40s, are huddled together and laughing. Part of their conversation catches my attention, especially when the youngest looking in the bunch starts talking.

"Yeah. He's such a weird doctor. He wears those bow ties and always seems to know when a patient is about to flatline."

Julia Caroline and I lock eyes. I motion for her not to say anything. *Hopefully, they'll keep talking … I've got to hear this!* We move a little closer, hiding behind a pillar, and the oldest of the nurses nods.

"One time, I walked in on him talking in an empty room. He gives me the creeps."

The young nurse who has helped Julia Caroline several

times nearly bumps into us in the hallway. "What are you two up to?"

My pulse is racing. "Sorry about that! I'm a little scattered right now. We were getting ready to take a walk. Can you let the rest of the nurses know?

She nods. "It's great seeing you out of bed, but you should be in a wheelchair if you're going further than the bathroom."

Julia Caroline smiles weakly but doesn't say a word, so I jump in.

"Thanks so much, but I'll make sure she doesn't fall. She has some other family visiting, so we may be gone for a while. Text me if you need us to come back for anything."

The nurse nods, and I thank her again before we move toward the elevator. While we're waiting, Julia Caroline pretends to wipe her brow.

"Whew! That was close! Do you think they were talking about Tom?"

"I think so, but does that mean he can communicate with the dead?"

Julia Caroline shrugs. "Anything is possible."

When the elevator door opens, we step inside, and I sigh. "Just so you're prepared, this is where the ghosts ambush me … almost every time I take the elevator." I didn't want to bring the mood down at all, but she may as well know what to expect.

Julia Caroline's eyes narrow, and she throws her hands up. "Dan doesn't want to mess with me today. I'll send him running toward the light for sure. Hell hath no fury like Granny Mason."

"Amen!" I grin. "On second thought, maybe we should turn you loose on him. I'd like to watch him squirm like the snake he is. After everything he put Mario and his family through and all my fretting over Clint's safety! Yep—an angry Julia Caroline Mason is what he deserves!"

Julia Caroline throws her head back laughing. My heart warms, and my cheeks hurt because I'm smiling so hard. *Oh goodness, how I needed to hear her one-of-a-kind laugh!*

We reach the first floor without any ghostly visitors popping out of the woodwork. *What a relief!* I follow Julia Caroline through the gift shop. She makes a beeline for the greeting card section, and we giggle while we flip through all the silly cards like we used to as girls at the Mount Pleasant Five and Dime. We may be old biddies now, but at least we've kept our wacky, sassy personalities all these years!

Out of the corner of my eye, I spot another blast from the past—some of the peach cordial hard candy we made in our high school home economics class during Christmastime. I have to buy that for the girls to try. I doubt they've ever had it.

As I line up to pay, Julia Caroline says she's a little weak and is going to sit down on the bench just outside the shop. Her face is looking mighty pale again.

I don't want to make a big deal out of it and stress her out, so I don't say anything. But this doesn't sit right with me. She's always been as strong as an ox. Well, she had surgery earlier today. Even a young spring chicken would be tired. *Oh, Lord—I hope that's all it is.*

A cold chill courses through my veins, and I rub my arms. *Dang!* Since Julia Caroline doesn't want her granddaughters to find out they might have clairvoyant abilities, we don't need any ghosts crashing the party. But it would be interesting to see if they see or hear anything out of the ordinary. Typically, most people need to experience a traumatic event before their abilities awaken. Considering their family's long history of communicating with the dead, these young ladies may be the exception to the rule.

As curious as I am, I don't want the Nelson sisters exposed to the constant harassment that comes with the irritating gift.

Just before it's my turn to pay, I hear a man and a woman yelling at each other outside the shop. I can't make out what they're saying, but I recognize their voices. My stomach drops as I think through who it might be. I drop the candy on the register stand, apologize to the cashier, and run out the door.

CHAPTER 21

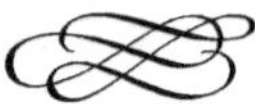

*E*xiting the shop, I look for the source of the disruption only to find Clint sitting alone on the bench with his head in his hands. *Oh, my stars! I forgot to tell him Blake would be in town!*

My heart aches…I'm guessing they had a fight, and Julia Caroline took the girls back upstairs. I hate making assumptions, though.

I sit down next to him and rub his back. "I'm so sorry I didn't give you a heads up about the girls heading this way. This has been one of the craziest times in my life, and I'm not thinking clearly."

He doesn't say anything but pulls his hands away from his face, revealing red, puffy marks under his eyes. My stomach drops. It's so unfair that these two youngsters weren't able to make their long-distance relationship work. They're meant for each other more than any couple I've ever met. I've tried so hard not to give up hope that they'll eventually come back around to one another.

Clint clears his throat. "It's not your fault. Blake overreacted to seeing me. That's all. I didn't say anything other than, 'hi,' before she freaked out. She really needs to chill."

"Yeah. She does. You don't deserve to be mistreated. Y'all broke up a long time ago, and you're adults. Julia Caroline and I want you here, but we don't need to add any more stress for anyone right now. I'll talk to Blake. I'm sure this won't happen again, hon. Why don't you head home and relax? I'll call you in the morning when we're ready to leave."

He nods, and I hug him.

"I love you, kiddo. Don't let this stress you out. If we can help Julia Caroline get through this nightmare, I'm going to take you and your brothers on a nice, long vacation. Start thinking about where we should go, and we'll ask the rest of the guys what they think."

"Okay. I love you, too. I'll think on it. See you tomorrow."

After he leaves, I go to the ladies' room and wash my face. *God, please provide us with the strength to deal with all these overwhelming emotions.*

My eye twitches a little bit, and I groan. Muscle spasms are the most irritating thing, especially when they involve your eyes! Looking in the mirror, I give myself a pep talk—chin up! Julia Caroline is going to be fine. Don't worry about Blake and Clint. They'll work it out and at least be able to tolerate each other. They don't have a choice in this family. It's not like they have to be around each other often, with them living six hours apart. Now, if I can convince Blake to drop the sass, we'll be in business!

Before I head up to Julia Caroline's room, I go to the cafeteria to buy some bottled drinks and snacks to share with everyone.

Then, I go to the elevator. Holding my breath, I pray for no ghostly visitors so that I can make it upstairs without any stressful events. But the iridescent film in the air tells me my wish won't be granted. I grit my teeth and prepare for the worst.

Thankfully, Mario appears a moment later. If Dan had

popped up instead, this elevator ride would have been much different.

He reaches out for me, and I gasp. "What are you doing?"

"Help me, please! Things are getting much worse in this in-between space I'm stuck in. I'm afraid of what Dan will try next. He's determined to hurt me, and I think he's getting closer to figuring out how to kill someone who is still alive. I'm so worried about what he will do to Lauren. He thinks they should be together."

"Oh, my lands! We won't let him do anything to your family. I'll check on them as soon as I'm upstairs. We're still cooking up a plan for good ol' Dan."

"Thank you! I wish I could do something myself. Having been a police officer for many years, I helped hundreds of people in danger. I feel so helpless not being able to protect my family. It's the worst."

"Hon, I'm sorry you're going through this. Julia Caroline is going home tomorrow. I promise I'll do my best to stop by your mom's place after she is settled."

He nods and vanishes into a silvery mist just as the elevator door slides open, revealing Tom and his red and blue polka-dotted bowtie. My heart begins pounding, and my palms start sweating. Goodness gracious—I don't know why. We've only talked a few times. I'm probably just startled because we keep running into each other right after I've had a ghostly encounter. Sheesh … there's no need to get worked up over nothin'.

His eyes light up. "Hey, you! I wondered where you were hiding." I freeze in place—was he really thinking about me? "I just swung by to chat with Mrs. Mason. She has a lovely crew of visitors in her room. Family is the best medicine."

"I totally agree. I was just picking up some provisions." I motion toward the bag of goodies.

"Great! Hope you enjoy a peaceful evening, and I'll see y'all in the morning."

I bid him goodnight and continue walking toward Julia Caroline's room. The girls are cuddled up on the sleeper chair, scrolling on their phones, and Julia Caroline is asleep again. I'm tempted to give Blake a piece of my mind, but this just doesn't feel like the right time. Instead, I pass the bag of treats to the girls and sign, "Help yourselves," hoping we don't wake Julia Caroline in the process.

Blake hangs her head low and signs, "Sorry for the drama." Her cheeks redden. "Did Clint leave?"

I nod and sign back, "Yep. He did." Maybe I should have stopped myself there, but I'm not good at keeping things to myself.

I steady my shaking hands. "Hon, we're all going through a lot right now. But what you don't know is that Clint also just lost his best friend and police partner. I'm not pointing fingers at either of you. I'm just asking you both to call a truce. Whatever we face will be easier if we don't hurt each other."

She purses her lips but nods. "I promise to behave myself. I didn't mean to lose my cool. It's just that's the first time I've seen him since we broke up, but I can keep the peace as long as he does. I'm really sorry to hear about his friend and partner. That must be hard."

I smile weakly. "Thanks, hon. I've already spoken to him. He won't give you any grief."

She gets up and squeezes me tight before whispering, "I love you," in my ear. I kiss her cheek.

Thank goodness she understands I didn't mean any harm. I wish I'd talked to both of them ahead of time, but I don't have a time machine. If I did, I'd go back in time a couple of years and warn Julia Caroline to pay closer attention to her health. While I'm daydreaming, I would rewind time and tell Wesley and MaryAnne not to go out to dinner the night of their fatal wreck. That's always my number one wish.

My phone dings—it's a text notification from Susan. She's about ten minutes away. Since Julia Caroline is asleep, I'm going to take the opportunity to caffeinate and meet her in the lobby. I tell the girls where I'm going and head that way.

The elevator ride is uneventful ... *thank the Lord!* A few minutes of quiet with a gallon of coffee is exactly what the doctor ordered.

Walking into the cafeteria, I grab two of the largest Styrofoam cups at the beverage station and fill them both nearly to the top. I save just enough space for a splash of cream and a sugar packet. Susan probably needs a boost after her drive, and if she doesn't, I'll drink her cup, too. I could probably drain the entire coffee urn by myself and still need more caffeine.

A display packed with pastries catches my eye, and I can't pass up the blackberry cobbler muffin, topped with brown sugar crumbles. I'm not dieting until Julia Caroline's health is in the clear. I've earned at least a few weeks of guilt-free gluttony. I picked out a cream cheese and peach filled tart for Susan and paid for our treats. Food is our love language in the Lowcountry. If anyone is hurting, we have to load them up with delicious comfort food.

I find a table in the cafeteria, sit down, and text Susan, asking her to meet me here.

I lie my head down, close my eyes, and say a silent prayer. "Dear Heavenly Father—I've asked for a lot lately, but I humbly pray that you bring Julia Caroline through this challenging time in her life unscathed and stronger for it. In Jesus' name, I pray. Amen."

CHAPTER 22

"Nan? Are you okay?" Of course, someone would see me in this state. Not that I'd ever be embarrassed about praying, but I probably look like I'm having a stroke with my head down on the table and whispering to myself. It's not a becoming look for anyone.

I look up to see Susan, and I jump to my feet and hug her tightly. I don't let go for a minute, and when I do, I tear up.

After I wipe my cheeks with a hanky, I clear my throat. "Oh, hon! It's been the absolute worst time of my life, but I think so. I was praying for your mom. I need her to be okay … more than anything. She just has to be! I believe God will heal her. It's just one of those obstacles we all have to face in life."

Tears roll down Susan's face. "I'm so worried, but I don't want Mom or the girls to see me cry."

My eye spasms start up again, and I massage my temples. "That's why I asked you to meet me here. We can be real with each other. She's scared me to death more than once this week. I'm trying to hold it together, but it ain't been easy. To make matters worse, Connie's son, Mario, was shot."

I go on to tell Susan about Mario's family and how he had

been working with Clint. I don't mention a word about our ghostly companions. Susan is a skeptic when it comes to the paranormal world. Julia Caroline has always said she believes clairvoyance skips a generation in her family. She inherited her abilities from her grandmother. That's why she anticipates her granddaughters' powers will awaken any day now.

She slaps her hand against her face and gasps. "Oh, my goodness! That is so awful! Poor Connie and Clint. I remember talking to Mario at Clint's birthday parties. He seemed like a great kid, and it sounds like he was a wonderful man."

"He was. Life can be so unfair and complex."

Susan sighs. "That's for sure."

"Speaking of complicated, Blake and Clint had a little run-in. I asked them to cool it, but I wanted to let you know." I shared what little background I had on what went down between them and reassured Susan that they seem okay now.

Susan's eyes widen. "Why on earth did they have to run into each other here? Blake wouldn't admit it, but she hasn't gotten over Clint—no guy ever measures up to him."

"It was my fault … I didn't warn Clint to stay away. I should have, but my head hasn't been screwed on tight this week." I sigh.

"I'm not blaming you. We're not ourselves right now, and you've been carrying the brunt of the stress for our family. We're here to help y'all now, so please give yourself some grace. Is Clint doing okay? It's been at least six months since we've talked."

"I believe he still loves her, too. He would never tell me that, but call it a grandmotherly instinct. I wish they would give it another go. They're so young and deserve to be happy."

Susan smiles. "It would be fantastic. I've always rooted for them to be together, but you know how stubborn they are. And Blake is dating someone, who I don't … well, I promised her I'd try to like him … but it isn't going well. There's something that's off about him. He sounds great on paper—he's a lawyer at his family law firm, owns a beautiful downtown loft apartment, and has a ton of friends. But then, some things he does or says upset her, and that doesn't sit well with Jeremy or me."

I groan. Susan and her husband, Jeremy, are the most open-minded, loving people. I've never heard either of them say they don't like someone. This young man must be a real bad egg. I'll have to talk to Blake soon. I don't want some loser to con our girl into ruining her life.

"That's awful. I hope she comes to her senses soon." I yawn hard. "Goodness. I guess I'm getting tired. Are you ready to go upstairs to see your mom?"

"Yeah. Do you want me to stay here with her tonight? I'm planning to send the girls to stock her house with groceries, and they can crash there. I'm sure you need to sleep after everything that's happened. I will call if anything comes up, but I doubt you'll even have to come back in the morning. It doesn't sound like the doctors will have the pathology reports for a bit."

"Sure. That works for me. I can come back if you need anything." As Susan and I walk toward the elevator, uneasiness rises in my chest and not just because I'm worried about bumping into a ghost.

We're taking Julia Caroline back home tomorrow, so why am I feeling so darn unsettled? I try pushing the bad energy out of my body. If I want everyone else to be positive, I should follow my own orders. Being a Negative Nancy never helps anyone, least of all myself. I've always hated that popular insult being connected to my name, so I make it a point to be cheerful and uplifting on the outside whenever I can, even if I think the most scathing thoughts.

When we reach Julia Caroline's room, she is asleep. I'd planned to say goodnight, but I don't want to wake her up. Instead, I wave to the rest of the ladies and blow them a kiss before returning to the elevator.

It doesn't seem right to leave, but my best friend is in good hands with her family. They need some time without me, even if we're wound together so tightly that I forget they aren't my blood-related kinfolk. Julia Caroline is the best sister in the world; that's for sure.

My phone rings—*it's Clint!* I duck into an empty waiting room to answer. When I greet him, he sighs.

"What's wrong, hon?"

"Some officers in West Ashley found Dan's car and body in the river a few days ago. You know the outage we had at my PD. Well, they use the same system and had a similar issue. That's why we hadn't heard anything about the accident."

"Oh, dear. Do you think we should tell Mario's family now?"

He gulps. "Yeah. Ugh—I guess I'll call her and Connie. I know it's getting late, but the news stations are running the story about the accident tonight. I'm going to ask Lauren to come forward and mention that he is a person of interest in Mario's murder. If we can find some evidence in his vehicle, it will put all our minds at ease knowing the killer is off the streets. But, Gram, I'm not going to tell anyone about this hocus-pocus business. If you want to, that's up to you."

My boy has taken some giant leaps toward being more open to the spiritual world, so I'm not complaining about his comments. We say goodnight, and I set a course for leaving the hospital again.

As I step onto the elevator, the door slams closed. That's odd —it's never done that before. The hair on my arm stands on end, and my heart is pounding in my throat.

The door opens just as hard as the elevator reaches the next floor, and no one is there. *Great! If I weren't ten stories up, I'd be tempted to get off and take the stairs instead. But the bones and muscles in my leg would turn into Jello before I made it to the bottom, so I guess I'm stuck on this death trap.*

"Hold the door!" A familiar voice calls out, and I press the door open button.

Tom comes running around the corner, panting. "Thank goodness it's you. Not too many people would have waited that long. I pressed the button and realized I'd forgotten my wallet in my office, just down the way. I'm in a huge hurry to leave. My dog walker couldn't let the pup out this afternoon, so Bruno is probably crossing his legs. Or he gave up and peed on my antique rug. Either way, I feel guilty for leaving him for eight or more hours every day. It's one of the hardest things about living alone."

"Poor fella. I thought you were leaving earlier."

He sighs. "I was, but I had an urgent call come in that I had to take. A lot can go sideways quickly on the oncology floor."

"I bet that's hard. I wouldn't handle all the bad news very well, especially when I had to tell the family members someone was dying. To be honest, I hate hospitals because they're a constant reminder of sickness and death. I'm only here because I love Julia Caroline more than life itself."

His eyes dim a little. Did I say something wrong? "You're a great friend. She's lucky to have you and the rest of her family rooting for her. Not all my patients have people who care about them. It really makes a difference when a patient is recovering."

"I read about that recently. We're all on board … whenever and whatever she needs. Hopefully, it will be smooth sailing after tomorrow."

Tom starts to say something, but the elevator jerks suddenly. I reach out for the wall to catch myself, but Tom loses his balance, knocking us onto the floor beside each other. I'm stunned for a moment and don't say anything. I turn my gaze to a wide-eyed Tom.

He pulls himself up and offers his hand to help me. "Well, that was certainly a surprise. Are you okay?"

I take his hands and manage to squeak out that I'm fine. When I'm on my feet, I notice how closely we're standing. It's been a while since I've stood less than a foot away from a man. He's staring at me, and I can't look away. Heat rises in my throat, and sweat beads up across my brow. *This is more terri-*

fying than any haunting—give me a malevolent spirit any day! I have a much better track record with ghosts!

As he leans in, my heart pounds furiously. He gently brushes my hair off my cheek and gives me the gentlest and sweetest kiss of my life. I didn't realize I'd been missing this sort of closeness with a man.

Maybe I was in denial.

The elevator door dings, and I turn to see who has joined us —no one. The door slams shut again. Weird. Something is up. If I had to guess, I'd put my money on Dan being the culprit. The elevator thrusts downward again and bounces slightly upward.

Tom groans. "Not again!"

"What's wrong? Please don't tell me we're stuck on here."

"I'm afraid so. I got stuck last week, and no one came to help for three hours. I called the administrator and told him that he's going to have to loosen the purse strings to fix his contraption. There's no choice anymore. A patient is going to get hurt or worse."

I start to agree with him, but in my peripheral vision, a silvery film builds in the corner. Please let it be Mario; he'll understand that I can't talk right now!

No such luck—Dan's evil face appears. I try ignoring him, but when I don't respond to his banter, he screams louder than a cat on the prowl. I'm only going to be able to tolerate this for so long. *Oh, good gravy!* I know what Julia Caroline and I overheard the nurses say about Tom acting weird. But he still doesn't strike me as the type to believe in what he'd probably call mumbo jumbo, hocus-pocus, or some other silly term for magical and paranormal things that can't be easily explained.

Tom pulls out his phone and says he's going to text for help. I hope they hurry this time. I won't survive Dan's nonsense much longer without putting the blooming idiot in his place.

CHAPTER 23

*D*an carried on for at least five minutes. In between screaming fits, he tells me about his plans to eliminate Mario's spirit and kill Lauren so that she can join him in this miserable land of nothingness. I desperately want to yell back and demand that he leave Mario's family alone—none of them wants anything to do with him. But I can't.

Tom sighs. "I've texted our property manager, the hospital administrator, and the repairman who saved my butt last time. I kept his phone number, just in case. Glad I did."

Hopefully, someone can help us soon. I know you're desperate to get home to Bruno. Poor guy."

"Yeah. I'm worried about him. My sister lives about an hour away. I texted her and asked if she could let him out. She's always looking for an excuse to go to the beach, but my brother-in-law hates it, so she jumped on the opportunity to stay the night at my house."

It's exceptionally hard to focus on what he's saying, but I'm trying my best to pretend that everything is normal.

I force a smile. "I'm pretty sure you don't live on Isle of

Palms. We would have bumped into each other at the grocery store or Acme by now. Which beach do you live on?"

"Oh, I'm just across Breach Inlet on Sullivan's Island. My housekeeper picks up my groceries on her way to clean my house every Monday morning, and I don't eat out very often. I'm usually at the hospital pretty long hours … probably the reason I've lived alone all these years. I never slowed down enough to do the whole husband and family thing. Now that I'm getting older, it's something I regret every day."

My heart sinks. "It's hard. I've been blessed as a mom and grandmother, but I've never had a great love story. My late ex-husband, my son's father, was abusive and controlling. He tried to hurt my son, and we got the heck out of dodge right then."

Tom doesn't respond.

"What's wrong?" He still doesn't say anything.

What the heck? Should I be worried? Nah—with the one-man … err … ghostly idiot show Dan is performing in the background, I can't focus enough to care about Tom's lack of interest. I'd rather not have to talk at the moment, anyway.

BINGO! I just figured out how to send Dan away without revealing my abilities to Tom.

"Hey, Tom. I believe in the power of prayer, and I'm going to recite the Lord's prayer. You're welcome to join in, but no pressure." This trick is starting to feel repetitive, but it's all I have until Julia Caroline and I can get back to her house.

He shivers. "I'm so sorry. I'm worried out of my mind about getting out of here and a few other things. I know you've been talking, but I haven't heard a word you have said. I didn't mean to be rude. There's no one else I'd rather be with now. I just wish we were sitting on my front porch with Bruno and a couple of tall glasses of sweet tea instead of stuck on this blasted elevator."

"That sounds peaceful. I was just saying I'm going to pray. The big guy upstairs always listens, even when no one else responds to texts."

He nods, and I start reciting the Lord's Prayer while holding my cross necklace.

Dan's screaming quietens a little at a time, and he disappears entirely into his trademark silverly mist. *Bye-bye, Danny Boy!* His obnoxious taunting chatter is still playing on repeat in my mind, and I can't wait until I can try Julia Caroline's idea to send him off to the Other Side. This farewell will be especially gratifying.

Tom snaps his head toward me. "How did you do that?"

"What are you talking about?"

"How did you get rid of that imbecile? I've never been exposed to such an annoying spirit in my life!"

My jaw drops—*the nurses were right!*

"Wait ... you can see and communicate with the dead?"

"Unfortunately, it's something I developed when my parents died. They're the only ones I saw for the longest time. When they crossed over, it's like the floodgates opened, and I've been drowning ever since. I see at least twenty every day at the hospital. I'm usually able to ignore them completely, but this worm has been popping up all week. I'd never seen him before, so he must have passed recently."

I frown. "Yeah. His name is Dan. He killed my friend's son, then he died in a stupid accident. You know the young police officer who was shot earlier this week?"

"Yes. That was so tragic."

"That's Connie's son. He left behind his lovely wife, Lauren, and their two-year-old tot, all because Dan was jealous."

"Oh, my. I can't fathom how Dan thought he'd be happy after killing someone to get what he wanted. Did he really think she would want to be with him after all that?"

"Some people ..."

Tom sighs. "So, how did you learn how to get rid of the horrible ones?"

"It's a very long story, but Julia Caroline figured things out a long time ago. My abilities are nothing compared to hers. But I can hold my own when sending them away temporarily. That's the bad news: Dan will come back. We're going to work on a more permanent fix when we get back to Julia Caroline's house tomorrow."

Tom raises his eyebrows. "I'm impressed. There's so much more to you and Julia Caroline than what meets the eye."

"Gee—thanks." I wink playfully.

He blushes. "You know what I mean. I think you're both outstanding women. I'm especially enjoying getting to know you."

It's my cheeks' turn to redden. Against my better judgment, I lean in to kiss him. I never make a move like this, especially at the beginning of a relationship or whatever this is. But what the hay? He wraps his arms around my neck, and a tingle runs down my spine, something that usually only happens when I have a ghostly hitchhiker. The scent of his woodsy cologne draws in my senses, and I desperately want to escape to a remote mountain cabin with him.

The kiss ends, and I have to steady myself. *Boy, howdy! This situation got a little out of control for a post-menopausal grandma. But, hey, it's good to know I've still got it.*

Tom grins widely. "All in all, I'm glad we got stuck in this elevator together. It would have taken me months to slow down at work long enough to grab coffee with you. By then, you'd probably be dating someone else, and I'd have no idea what I was missing. That would have been a real shame."

I snort. "You overestimate my romantic prospects. You're the first in years."

"I find that very hard to believe."

He kisses me again. This kiss is less heart-attack-inducing than the other two, which is good because the elevator door opens with a loud clank.

The repairman and a young couple on the other side of the door clap. Tom takes a bow, and I just laugh. Hopefully, I'll never bump into this elevator repairman again. I don't think I could keep a straight face.

As for the couple, the woman is clearly about to pop any minute now. They're probably headed for labor and delivery. They won't remember this story after their little miracle arrives. Even if they do, maybe our performance will inspire them to grow old together. I want that for everyone, even though I've never experienced it.

Tom and I may not have spent the past few decades together, but we can enjoy all the moments we have now. Who knows what the future will bring?

As we head toward the parking lot, the stars shine brightly, and Tom grabs my hand. It might be hot and sticky outside, but I don't care. My heart is full for the first time in a while. I love my family and friends, but there's nothing like a bit of old-fashioned romance.

The glow of the streetlights illuminates the walkway as he walks me to my car. *Thank goodness!* Otherwise, I wouldn't be able to see the way he's looking at me. It takes my breath away. I always thought swooning was just a pile of bull hockey … just a phrase that women of weak character used when making up an excuse for their indiscretions.

I was wrong—I could kiss this man all day! I won't be doing anything more than kissing unless I'm wearing a wedding band on my left hand.

When we reach my car, Tom kisses my hand.

"I'm so glad we spent the evening together, even though it was under bizarre circumstances. We'll go on a proper date soon."

"It's been a lovely but strange night. I'm looking forward to it."

He caresses my cheek with his hand and leans in for another perfect kiss. I may be floating off the pavement. So much for getting a solid night of sleep after all this excitement! I don't want to leave, but we need to go our separate ways. Before I get into my car, I write my phone number down on a scratch piece of paper from my purse and hand it to him.

Even though he's in a rush, he pulls out his cell phone and calls me on the spot.

"Now you have my number, too. Have a wonderful evening, beautiful."

Forget the streetlights—I can feel myself glowing from the inside out. I bet astronauts in space can see me sparkling a million light-years away in a hospital parking lot in Mount Pleasant, South Carolina.

We finally say our last round of goodbyes, and I head for the highway. In the South, we can't ever leave right after the first goodbye, especially if it's someone we enjoy being around. I can't believe I'm falling for the man I was mocking and calling Dr. Bow Tie just a couple of days ago. Romance is such a strange and complex beast. But I ain't complainin'!

Pulling into my driveway, I barely remember the drive home, but somehow, I made it in one piece. What a day! Wait until I tell Julia Caroline about everything! She is going to have a fit!

I pad barefoot through my kitchen to retrieve my slippers and fix a cup of peach tea, which I take upstairs to my bedroom. Sinking into my bed, I close my eyes and daydream about Tom and me going on our first proper date.

Where should we go? The beach or a park? Probably not … it's too hot right now if you aren't swimming, and I'm not ready to wear a bathing suit in front of him. Besides, the mosquitoes have taken over Charleston County for the season, and getting sand blown into your mouth isn't exactly romantic. Maybe we could go out to dinner and watch a movie. Hmm … we wouldn't be able to talk during a movie, so that's a bad idea. On the other hand, it would be nice to cuddle up together and share a big bucket of buttery popcorn. I'm sure we'll come up with something fun.

Whether it's the tea or the rush of a new romance, I feel completely relaxed for the first time this week. I pull up my coverlet, tuck my hand under my pillow, and drift off into a deep sleep.

CHAPTER 24

The sound of my phone ringing wakes me, but I can't shake my sleepiness. Is it the middle of the night? I glance over at my alarm clock—it's 8:30. By my standards, I slept in a little. I needed the shut-eye, but it's definitely time to pull my booty out of bed. I roll over to answer the call and let out a loud yawn.

What if Tom is on the other end of the line? I should have checked my caller ID. I'm not used to trying to impress someone.

Julia Caroline's laugh fills my bedroom, and I let out a sigh of relief. *Whew!*

"Oh, thank the good Lord it's you! I was fit to be tied! I don't know what I woulda done if it wasn't!"

"Who were you expecting, Tom?"

"Maybe." I giggle and fill her in on my elevator escapade with Tom. "We haven't even been on a real date yet, but I'm as giddy as a schoolgirl. I'd forgotten how fun kissing and flirting can be."

"Oh, Nan! It's the best. I miss my James something fierce sometimes. I'm glad you've found a man. I thought Brian was going to be the one, but he moved just when y'all were getting close."

"You know how much I miss James, but you might find someone new, too. There's still time."

"Nah—I'm good. We were together too long. I'd always picture him when I was kissing someone. It wouldn't be fair for me to put anyone through that mess."

"Well, you might change your mind if you meet the right person. Not to change the subject, but why were you calling? Are you busting out of the joint this morning? Do you want me to come to the hospital?"

"Nope. I just signed my discharge papers, and Susan is going to bring me home. Wanna meet us back at my place? The girls are picking up breakfast from Acme. I told them to order enough for you and Clint. And before you ask, Blake told me she went off on Clint. She feels terrible about it. It was her idea to invite him to join us. He's more than welcome … as always. You're both our family."

I'm so proud of Blake for owning up to her fiery temper and offering an olive branch to Clint. She comes by it honest—Julia Caroline can be a pistol when she wants.

"Nan? You still there?"

"Yep. Sorry. I had something caught in my throat. I'll definitely be there. I'm not sure what Clint's work schedule is today, but I'll ask him to come over."

"Great! And Nan?"

"Yeah?"

"Thanks for supporting me through all this. I would have been so lonely if you hadn't been around. I love you."

I force the tears that threaten to escape my eyes to stay put. I need to reply, but I don't want to become a blubbering mess. Today is a good day, and I've cried enough lately. Finally, I regain my composure.

"I love you, too. You can't ever scare me like this again. I want to be front porch sittin' with you until we're at least a hundred years old. Got it?"

"I'll do my best."

I smile. "I'm glad we're on the same page. Now get yourself home from the hospital in one piece, you hear? I'm going to run by Connie's really quick, and I'll head over to your place."

"Tell Connie's family I said 'hi.' I'd love to see them, especially little Georgie. He's such a cutie pie."

We say our goodbyes, and I freshen up for the day. Running a comb through my hair is easier said than done, but I finally work out all the knots. Sleeping on the pullout chair at the hospital didn't do my tangled rat's nest any favors. I pick out a brightly colored blouse with tan linen slacks. I get dressed, dab on a bit of makeup, and glance in the mirror. Not half bad for a sixty-seven-year-old grandma. What would Tom think about this outfit? Maybe I could wear it on our date.

I focus on gathering everything I need to leave the house. As I lock the front door, I can't shake the feeling that someone is watching me. But there isn't a soul, dead or alive, in sight.

"Mario, is that you? If you can't show yourself right now, can you give me some sort of sign?"

Nothing.

I grit my teeth and ball my fists. "Dan. If that's you, I don't have time for your shenanigans. Please save me the trouble of pulling out my cross and putting you in your place. Today ain't the day, Sugar!"

Crickets.

Fine. I sigh. Something is afoot, but I don't want to waste any more time. I haven't been able to visit Connie's family as much as I'd like. They've gotta be struggling, but next to my boys, Julia Caroline is my priority. At least Connie and Lauren have each other.

I get into my car and make the short drive over to Connie's house. Something isn't right, but until whoever wants my attention shows their face, I can't do much.

When I pull into the driveway, Lauren is kneeling in the flowerbed, pulling weeds. She wipes a bead of sweat from her brow and waves.

"Hey, hon. Are you doin' alright?"

"Most of the time. The news of Dan's death was a mixed blessing. I feel in my bones that he was involved in Mario's death, but I can't prove it." She wipes a tear from her eye. "When Clint called last night, he asked me to call his Chief and file a report about Dan following us here from California."

I grab her hand. "You should. That would give the police more of a right to look for evidence that would confirm Dan was the killer. I'm sorry you're having to deal with all this. Is everything else okay?"

"Well, I'm worried about Georgie. He keeps saying he has a friend, but we haven't taken him anywhere except the grocery store. I guess it's normal for kids to have imaginary friends, but with his new ... um ... ability, I'm concerned about what may be going on. It's not like I can see ghosts to know if there's one around. I like imagining it's Mario watching out for him, but now that I know about Dan, I can't help but worry that he's trying to hurt us from beyond the grave. He can't, though, right?"

I so badly want to say, "Wrong, Sugar Pie. The devil himself walks this earth. Be on guard at all times." Of course, I don't want to worry her, so I keep my lips sealed. My heart races, but I force a weak smile. "I'll take a look and pay close attention to what Georgie is up to."

She lets out a deep exhale. "Thank you so much. A mama's mind and heart never get a break. I want him to be safe and happy. That's really all that matters to me."

"Believe me—I understand, hon. You're doing a great job with him. Where is he now?"

Lauren leads the way into the house and upstairs to Mario's childhood bedroom. Nirvana and Grateful Dead posters deck the walls, and a disco light rests on a high shelf. Georgie is lying asleep in his pack-and-play, and this 1990s era time capsule feels like a strange nursery for a toddler. But I'm sure Connie couldn't bear to remove Mario's personal belongings.

I know that feeling all too well. I'll never forget dismantling Wesley's bedroom when I sold my house to move into his and MaryAnne's home with their children. It was one of the hardest things I've done in my life. But it was the right thing to do for Clint and his brothers. They didn't need to go through yet another change.

Something moves by Georgie's pack-and-play, and I brace myself for whatever comes next. I can hear what sounds like footsteps, but don't see anyone. *Golly ... are we doing this again? I'm too old for this crap!* I don't want to freak out Lauren until I'm sure there's something spooky afoot.

I move closer to the pack-and-play and peer into the dark corner. Two eyes glow back at me. Then, a purr rumbles from the corner. *Wait a minute—it's Connie's fluffy black cat, Persephone!*

She jumps out of the corner and hisses. *Dang old cat!*

Lauren groans. "I don't love her being in here with Georgie alone, but she seems to want to protect him. I've been trying to figure out why."

I shudder. Animals can often see spirits even when humans are oblivious to their presence. I bet Persephone picked up on ghostly activity and has been watching out for the tot. What can I do to draw out whoever is hiding here without worrying Lauren and Connie too much?

Lauren gently wakes Georgie, and he wipes his eyes. She kisses his forehead, and he smiles a wide grin, showing his five teeth. (At almost two, generally, children have more than five teeth. All seven of my children had around fifteen teeth at that age.) I loved how cute my boys looked at this age, but helping a toddler get through the teething phases ain't for the faint of heart. When he sees me, he waves with both hands and giggles.

"Hey, little one. I've missed you! Julia Caroline has, too, and she will come see you very soon."

He squeals and starts singing a baby gibberish song. This is so precious.

The sound of glass breaking catches my attention, and I turn around to see that the bedroom window has been broken. I ask Lauren to take Georgie out of the room so I can pick up the glass. But I really want to figure out what or who broke it.

I don't see a rock or stray tree limb, but nothing adds up when ghosts are involved.

CHAPTER 25

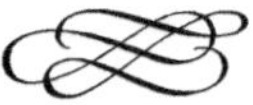

$\mathcal{A}$s I clean up the shards of glass, a repetitive tapping on the hardwood floors grabs my attention. *Ugh ..what now?* I lock my gaze on the whitewashed wooden rocking chair in the corner. Sure enough, it's moving back and forth, seemingly on its own. I couldn't be that lucky, though.

"Mario, is that you?"

There's no answer, but a silvery haze materializes, swirling in an iridescent glow near the window. A cold chill runs down my arms, and goosebumps pop up. While the blob solidifies into a human-like shape, I hold my breath.

Dan's face appears—I want to scream, but Lauren and Connie would probably come check on me. And I don't want to put them in danger or need to explain why I'm freaking out.

"Hey, Grandma. Why are you here?"

"To kick your sorry butt," I whisper.

There's no point in getting too fancy with the spell this time since Julia Caroline has longer-lasting plans for Dan. Besides, I can't take too long with Connie and Lauren waiting, so I recite the first Bible verse that comes to mind and hold out my cross pendant. Dan's apparition spirals into nothingness.

I catch my breath and continue cleaning up the debris.

How often does this jerk snoop on Lauren and Georgie? I don't like this one bit. I carefully pick up the remaining glass pieces, place them in a small metal garbage can in the upstairs bathroom, and close the door tightly behind me.

When I return to Georgie's room for one more quick scan for glass shards, an iridescent bubble forms. My heart palpitates —*is Dan coming back already?* He's never returned so quickly. I clench my jaw and brace myself for round two.

Mario appears, and I let out a deep exhale. *Praise the Lord!*

"Boy, am I happy to see you instead of hateful ol' Dan! I was worried he was coming back."

"I'm glad he's not here right now, too. I finally got through. I don't know where he goes, but every time he disappears for a bit, it's like a massive cinder block has been lifted off my shoulders. Did you figure out how to send him away forever?"

"Julia Caroline has an idea, and we're going to think about it today once she's home from the hospital. Listen, hon, focus your energy on staying here to watch over your family. If Dan shows up, take him on a wild goose chase over to Palm Court. We'll take it from there. Sound like a plan?"

"Yep. Got it. Thanks for helping protect my family."

"Of course, kiddo. Anytime."

After he disappears into a silvery mist, I pick up the remaining glass pieces, place them in a small metal garbage can in the upstairs bathroom, and close the door tightly behind me.

Now that I've checked on Connie's family, I need to get over to Julia Caroline's house. I go downstairs to tell the ladies about my conversation with Mario and let them know where I disposed of the glass. I can only imagine how badly Georgie would get hurt if he snuck off to the bathroom undetected.

Lauren clutches her chest. "You don't know how grateful I am to know it was Mario with Georgie." She grows quiet for a moment. "It's hard to comprehend, and I miss him so much. But it does me good to know he's still with us in some way, even if it's just for a little while."

Connie wipes a tear from her cheek, tugging at my heart. "It's such a blessing, but I know he can't stay forever. Do you think he can hear us if we want to say our goodbyes to him?"

I nod. "He sure can. He's trying to visit as much as possible, so if you think of something, just start talking. Chances are, he will hear most of what you say. I need to go over to Julia Caroline's house, but I'll come back when I can."

They thank me, and we say our goodbyes. Georgie toddles over and hugs my leg.

Lauren smiles. "I think he's adopted you as a surrogate grandma. He could always use another one. Come to think of it, I don't think anyone could have too many grandmothers to spoil and love them."

"I'm honored. I already care so much about him." My heart warms, and I grin. It's funny how people who aren't your blood relations can become part of your extended family in a matter of days.

After I get into my car, I make the quick three-minute drive to Julia Caroline's place. When I arrive, the string of parked cars and the sound of laughter coming through the beach cottage's open windows tell me the house is full of people and love. This is the best get-well gift for Julia Caroline. She's the happiest when her children and grandchildren visit. Most mamas and grandmamas are just that way. It's natural.

I'm beyond grateful Clint lives nearby, but when his brothers come home, there ain't nothin' better than having all my boys under one roof at the same time.

I park my car and stroll up the sand-and-shell drive to the front door, then let myself into the house.

"Hey, everyone! I'm here." Considering the volume of the chatter in the kitchen, I doubt anyone noticed me. I walk back to see Blake and Brittany's faces and hands covered in flour. I shake my head and grin. "Did you get any of that stuff in the bowl?"

Blake smirks and throws a fistful of flour at my face. "Welcome to the party!"

"Oh, it's on now, young lady!" I grab the sack of flour from her hands and lift it over her head.

"You wouldn't dare."

I raise my eyebrows. "I wouldn't? Are you sure about that?"

Elaina grabs the sack from me. "Stop messing around, y'all! This is the last flour in the house, and I need it to make Granny Mason some biscuits."

Blake shoves her hand deep into the flour sack and throws a hefty dose at Elaina's face, nailing her right on the nose and cheek. I try not to laugh when Elaina hollers because I know she's ready to kill Blake. It's funny how different these sisters are at times.

I hear the front door open a moment later, and I start walking toward the living room to see who's there.

"We're home, everyone," Julia Caroline calls out. Oh, lawdy—she's going to have a fit when she sees the state of this room. I run back to the disaster area where every surface and woman is covered in flour, but there's no time to clean up the mess. At least we're having fun.

When Julia Caroline enters the kitchen, her eyes widen. "What on earth have y'all been up to? I didn't realize you were going to destroy my house while I was at the hospital."

Blake gives her a sheepish grin. "We're cooking you a homemade breakfast."

She looks at her watch. "It's almost noon, so I guess we're eating brunch. Did any of the flour actually make it into the biscuits and gravy or whatever you're making, other than a mess?"

She winces. "Not yet."

Is Julia Caroline really mad? I cough to cover a laugh, just in case.

She gasps. "Y'all are too much. Why don't you just clean up and go pick up something from Acme like your mom asked in the first place?" She looks over at me. "And just how did you get pulled into this silliness?"

I shrug. "I just got here and was promptly greeted with this lovely makeup job."

Julia Caroline laughs so hard that her eyes start watering, and she is shaking so furiously that she has to sit down. Of course, I'm not one to let her laugh alone. I know I look ridiculous. When I regain my composure, I tell her to go rest while I help the girls clean up the mess. Somehow, I imagine this is going to go down as one of our favorite memories.

As my best friend leaves the kitchen, I notice her skin is still ashen, and she has lost even more weight and muscle than I'd originally thought.

My stomach drops—*how did I miss these clear signs of illness? Is she even worse off than we thought? Please, God, help her get strong and healthy again.*

Blake puts her arm around me, and I pat her hand. It's so wonderful that these girls came to visit. Julia Caroline and I both need them here with us, especially this week. They keep us young and provide the best kind of distraction from our problems. I wish they could visit more often, but it's good they have full lives with school and work. Susan and Jeremy have done a tremendous job raising these girls. I wonder where life will take them next.

Elaina claps her hands. "Alright. Let's get this place cleaned up, so we can go chill out."

I salute. "Yes, ma'am!" She ignores my sass, but the other two girls giggle.

While we clean the kitchen, Brittany leaves to pick up our food from Acme. *Dang! I should have volunteered to do that instead.* Cleaning up flour is always such a darn, goopy mess. It turns into a paste when you add water, and sweeping it just spreads little puffs around the room. Why didn't Blake throw corn flakes or spaghetti sauce, anything other than this bag of White Lily self-rising flour? Good thing none of us is gluten intolerant, or we'd be sick for sure.

After the kitchen is spic and span, the three of us join Susan in the living room. Julia Caroline must be in her bedroom. *Did she actually listen to me when I told her to relax? I guess there's a first time for everything.*

I excuse myself, wander upstairs, and knock on Julia Caroline's door. "Hey. I'm coming in."

When I open the door, she is out cold. I walk over to her bed and sit down next to her, like I've done many times. Memories of when she was on bed rest during her pregnancies, as well as the first few months after James died, come to mind. But support isn't a one-way street. She tends to me when I'm suffering and pulls me out of a funk more times than I can count. It's just what you do for your sisters.

I gently shake her awake. "Hey, lady. Brittany should be back with our food soon. Do you feel up to coming downstairs, or do you want me to bring you a plate?"

Julia sits upright. "I'll come down. Before I forget, let me grab my pearls for you." She stands and slowly pads over to her dresser, where she retrieves the necklace from her jewelry box.

When she hands them to me, I grimace. "Are you absolutely sure you're okay with me using them?"

"Of course. Why wouldn't I be? You and Connie's family are in danger. Keeping you safe is more important than any old piece of jewelry, family heirloom or not. Besides, I'm not likely to wear them anytime soon. Sick people don't go out on the town much."

"Stop it! You're going to get better. No—scratch that; you're already on the mend. You'll be shipshape again in no time. When you're up to it, we're going to have a huge party on the beach to celebrate. Then, we'll pack up for a fun getaway. It's going to be the wildest trip of our lives, so go ahead and buckle up for that!"

She smiles weakly. "That would be nice." Her smile fades, and she coughs. "Listen, you need to use the pearls tomorrow as close to midnight as you can. The shape of the pearl mimics that of the moon, which will be at its fullest then. And … well, never mind … it's just the best time. Don't ask me why; it just is."

"And what? Tell me, dang it all, woman!" I throw my hands in the air.

"It's nothing. Just find a way to get Dan to your house tomorrow right before midnight and use my pearls while reading this incantation." She hands me a folded notecard.

I take the card and frown. "Why am I using pearls? What's so special about them, I mean, other than they were your grandma's? I don't understand why you're being so weird."

She holds her finger up to her mouth. "Listen, babe, don't worry your pretty little head about a thing. They're powerful because my family has been adding a pearl to the strand at key life events for decades. If you do what the card says, it will work. So, just do it for me, okay?"

I shrug. "Alright … if you say so. This is really bizarre, and for us, that is saying something."

"Hush your mouth, lady, and just do it." She lies down again and turns her back to me. "I'm feeling exhausted and need a little more shut-eye. Y'all go ahead and eat. I'll set an alarm and come down in a little while."

I swallow hard. *Wow. She hasn't ever been this insistent or secretive about anything. What is going on?* I trust her more than life itself, so I have to believe she is giving me the best advice possible.

Why does it feel like she's pushing me away right now? I don't like any of this, not one bit.

CHAPTER 26

After we finish eating, we play a few rounds of cards on the screened-in porch. Julia Caroline pokes her head out the screen door and says she's fixing a plate to bring out with her. It's good to see her up and moving around, and she needs to pack on some fat to get stronger. I don't remember seeing her this thin since we were girls.

When she comes outside, she sits on the bench beside the table where we're playing our game and eats two bites of the shrimp and grits before setting her fork down again. I want to shove spoonfuls of grits and gravy down her throat, even if I have to force-feed her one calorie at a time.

"Why are you staring at me, Nan?"

"Just wondering why you're eating like a bird. You didn't have breakfast or lunch, and it's nearly dinnertime."

"I'm not hungry, but I'm trying to make myself eat something."

I decide to drop the subject, but my hands tremble so hard I have to set my cards down on the table. *What if she is too weak to recover from the cancer? What will I do? What will these girls do? I have to get through tomorrow night, and then, I'm going to stick to my best friend like a fly trying to walk through molasses until the doctors cure her.*

Blake holds up her cards and nods in my direction. "It's your turn."

I yawn. "I think I'm done. My brain has taken a leave of absence, and there's no hope of getting it back into the game. Why don't you deal with your granny in my place?"

Julia Caroline wrinkles her nose. "Ugh. You know I don't like playing card games." Her face relaxes. "Okay. Fine. Deal me in."

Blake hands Julia Caroline a stack of cards, and she sticks her tongue out at me.

I giggle. After watching them play a hand, my thoughts turn to what I'm in for with sending Dan to his final destination. I have no idea what to expect or how to prepare for this adventure. I trust my best friend, but that doesn't mean this isn't scary.

When Julia Caroline wins, I clap and whoop. Glancing down at my cell phone, I notice the time—it's almost 9 o'clock now. *Man, time flies!* I'd better go and craft some semblance of a plan before the turkey buzzard shows his ugly face tomorrow.

I take a big stretch and yawn again. "Hey—I'm going to head out for the night. I can see you're going to have a barrel of laughs tonight. Call if you need anything. Love y'all!"

When everyone says "bye," Julia Caroline slowly rises from her seat, announcing she is going back to bed. Before she heads upstairs, she leans in to give me a tight hug and whispers. "Love you. Good luck with everything. You're gonna do great! I have complete faith in you. I'll be seeing you soon."

"Oh, I'll see ya in the mornin'. I'm just going home to hash out a plan for tomorrow evenin'."

I'm glad she's confident in my abilities. I just wish I knew more about what to expect.

I haven't sent a spirit away for good without her. It's overwhelming to say the least, but Dan doesn't want to cross me.

I've made up my mind to do whatever it takes to send his sorry butt over to the Other Side ... Lord willing.

I say goodbye to everyone for the second time and walk out to my car. The nearly full moon illuminates the street. On any other night, I would stroll along the beach and take in the beautiful reflections on the ocean. Tonight, I'm grateful for the moon's magic, which can only help banish Dan to the Other Side.

A few moments later, I pull into my driveway, park quickly, mindlessly fumble for my house key and go inside.

How am I going to draw Dan here tomorrow? It's time to read the notecard—my pulse races. Two weeks ago, I didn't anticipate any of the horrors that have come our way – Mario's death, Julia Caroline being diagnosed with cancer, or Dan unleashing his terror on our loved ones. I don't know why any of these things have happened. I try not to question God; it's just hard to see people you care about hurting.

Drawing in a deep breath, I sit down on the living room sofa. As I unfold the notecard, I start reading the message from Julia Caroline.

Nan,

It's not fair that you're alone this time. I know you'll kick Dan's hind end real good, and these pearls have the power to help you. For almost a century, the women in my family have added a pearl to our necklace at every major life event—one for each baby, wedding, and death—impacting their immediate family. Before I gave you my necklace this morning, I added my last pearl, hoping to give you as much power as possible.

Grandmama said to always add the pearls on the day before a full moon and wear the necklace when you're ready to send a malevolent spirit to the Other Side. If you can align this day with a life event, all the better. Just before midnight on the night of the full moon, lead the spirit toward an open blue glass bottle and repeat the incantation below as many times as needed until the haint has taken up residence inside.

Bottling spell incantation: *To "bottle" their essence, simply lead them to a place they love or near a person they care about. Find an object in which you can trap them and say, "Leave the earth for a short while, gravitate in this object. This is not your final destination."*

To finish up, cork the bottle and recite a Bible verse. This will hold them in place overnight. When you wake the next morning, the spirit will have moved on to the hereafter.

My grandmother said the new pearl's powers would only work once. So, make it count. Protect our family and friends so y'all can live happy, safe lives together. I'll be seeing you soon.

Love,

Julia Caroline

WHAT? *Why does she sound like she's packing her bags and leaving to move across the globe? I don't get it. What is she hiding from me?* I pick up my cell phone, ready to yell at my best friend for scaring me. But it's getting late. I've been more than supportive and patient this past week. Right now, she is confusing and scaring me. She's the person I trust the most, but nothing has been normal lately. I really can't handle too much more craziness. After tomorrow night, I'm taking a break from chaos.

My phone rings in my hand, and I almost drop it. *What are the odds of that happening?* I check the caller ID—it's Susan. I answer the phone, and there is silence. *Great ... the island's cell towers don't always get the best connection, especially if it's windy outside.*

"Hey, Susan, are you there? Can you hear me?"

Muffled sounds come across the line. Did she butt-dial me by mistake?

"Susan. I'm hanging up. Call me back if you need anything."

"No!" She clears her throat. "Wait!" This can't be good.

"Hon, you're worrying me. What's wrong?"

"Mom's gone."

"What do you mean, gone?" My chest tightens, and I place my hand over my heart. *Oh, please, God—please don't let this mean what I think it does.*

Through Susan's crying in the background, I try to process what she just said. My brain is stuck like a broken record, playing back, "Mom's gone" over and over again. I don't feel like my mind and body are connected right now. *Maybe I'm having an out-of-body experience. I must have bumped my head, and this whole call is a delusion.*

Susan's pained voice brings me out of this strange dreamlike state. "Nan? I'm hurting somethin' fierce. What are we going to do?"

"I don't know," I whisper. "Have you told the girls yet?"

"Yeah … they're in bad shape." She sniffs. "We all are."

Julia Caroline Mason's death will have ripple effects across our families for a long time. My best friend made the most mundane moments seem magical. I know her family would agree. She was never content to let her girls' birthdays or any other milestone go by without celebrating.

"Do you want me to come over now?"

Susan sighs. "No. I still need to call for an ambulance. After they leave, I'm going to try to calm the girls down. This has been such a roller coaster of emotions for all of us. I may take something to help me sleep tonight. If I don't, I'll be an even bigger disaster tomorrow."

"Let me know if you want me to come over, and I'll be right there."

"Thanks, Nan. Love you."

"Love you, too, hon. I don't know how, but we'll get through this together."

We end our call, and I throw my hands up in the air. *"Why, God? I don't get it. I was supposed to grow old with my best friend! Why did you take her from me so soon?"*

I plop down on the couch, my thoughts spiraling from

begging for there to be some horrible mistake, or maybe I'm in a coma and having some weird fever dream. Reconciling with the fact that this is my reality isn't an option.

That lady was a life force. *Will I wither away without her? No, Clint and Julia Caroline's girls wouldn't let that happen. God love 'em.*

Clint! He doesn't know yet. My hands tremble as I dial his number.

When he picks up, I can't stop crying.

"Gram—are you okay?"

I take a series of shallow breaths. "Julia Caroline is gone."

"What? No!" Clint mutters something under his breath. "When?"

I cough. "Earlier tonight."

"That's unreal. I really thought she'd be okay after going through some treatments."

"Me too, hon."

"Gram, do you want me to come over? I'm at work, but I can get someone to cover for me and be there in twenty minutes or so."

I can't ask him to leave work, and I really just need to be alone. "No, sweetie. Just be careful out there. I'll see you tomorrow."

We say our goodbyes, and I can't stop fidgeting with my hands. *What the heck am I supposed to do now?*

For some reason, I turn on the TV and mindlessly click through the channels. The actors' words don't make sense as I flip through several shows. After a while, I zone out, and eventually my body gives in to sleep.

I dream Julia Caroline is still alive and well. We're laughing and dancing to Disco music while driving down the South Carolina coastline. The sun kisses our bare shoulders, and we're having the time of our lives until she drives her prized Thunderbird into a burning building, and the car explodes.

When I wake up, I'm covered in sweat. *What a horrifying nightmare!*

CHAPTER 27

Out of the corner of my eye, I see a silver glow start to form. I let out a guttural scream and jump to my feet. *Not now!* I don't want to entertain any spirits, but if I have to, I hope Mario will be the one to show up. He'll understand that I'm not up to talking.

A familiar navy-blue floral dress appears. I'm guessing this isn't Dan or Mario visiting me. I scratch my head. *Who is this?* I can't put my finger on why I recognize that pattern. When the spirit materializes, I go face blind. I know it's a woman, but I can't distinguish her features. Has she fully formed? *Who is this lady, and what does she want from me?* I start to tell her to leave me alone, but something tells me I shouldn't.

"Nan! Don't act like you don't know me." My best friend is standing in front of me, wearing her favorite dress, the one she wore when she and James renewed their vows months before he died.

I freeze in place. *No—it's not Julia Caroline. I'm dreaming again.* I rub my eyes.

"Nan! Don't ignore me. I don't know how long I'll get to stay. Remember, this is my first time being on this side of things."

I fall to my knees and double over, crying. "I can't go on without you. You're the only person who understands me. We're supposed to grow old together and watch our grandchildren find their places in life. How could you just give up?"

"Oh, Nan, it was just my time. I didn't give up. My grandmother's spirit came to me today and told me this was all settled a long time ago. Listen, go to my house tomorrow. In my jewelry box, you'll find a letter that explains everything."

I'm resisting the urge to pitch the biggest hissy fit of my life and run around my house screaming at the top of my lungs nonstop until I pass out, but I've gotta pull myself together to kick Dan's butt tonight. If I don't, I'm putting the people I love at risk. My window of opportunity is narrow to say the least. I wipe my eyes and nose on my sleeve … something I've always sworn that I'd never do. But, today, I don't give a rat's patootie if it's ladylike or not.

Julia Caroline frowns. "That's just plain disgusting, but I'm gonna give you a pass here. I'm sorry you're having to deal with this, but hopefully, the timing will work out in your favor. You needed a life event."

If she weren't dead, I'd choke her. "How could you say that? I would rather put up with Dan for the rest of my life than to lose you."

Closing my eyes, I pray I'll wake up and realize I ate a bad clam that caused this vivid nightmare to play out in such a horrific way. But I know it's my reality.

When I open my eyes, Julia Caroline is gone. *Where did she go?*

Ghosts never stick around 24/7, but her leaving without saying goodbye stings like pouring salt into all the wrong wounds. I let myself cry good and hard. This losing your best friend business ain't for the faint of heart. Whether I want to or not, I have to pull myself together. After I destroy Dan, I'll have to accept the death of the dearest lady on this side of Heaven.

First things first—I need to go see Susan and the girls and

read the blasted letter. I freshen up and change my clothes before leaving for Julia Caroline's house.

During my walk, the gray cloud-filled sky and light sprinkle mirror my mood. The gross weather means I don't have to watch smiling families carrying colorful umbrellas and coolers down the beach access path today.

Happiness is for the birds. Scratch that—I hate birds—they can be depressed, too.

Approaching Julia Caroline's house, the shell and sand driveway crunches under my feet. I take in the weathered beach cottage. She has aged with grace and beauty, with only a few blemishes in her whitewashed siding, black shutters, and neatly manicured landscaping.

The wide front porch welcomes me. But that doesn't mean much since my best friend, at least in her human form, won't be inside.

I knock on the door and announce myself as I enter. Julia Caroline's essence is everywhere. It seems like she is bound to pop out of the kitchen at any minute to greet me with a glass of sweet tea and her lovely smile. Those days are gone.

Elaina joins me in the living room and plops down on the sofa without saying a word.

I don't know what to say either, so I sit down next to her. She rests her head on my shoulder, and I pat her tear-stained cheek. *This isn't fair.* We had no time to prepare for Julia Caroline's death, not that a year or even twenty years would have kept us from grieving. I don't think my best friend fully appreciated how much we loved her. I guess no one can grasp the lasting impact they make on their circle of friends and family.

Susan pokes her head out of the kitchen door. The bags under her eyes don't surprise me. I doubt any of us slept well last night. She leans down to hug me, and I suppress tears. I don't want to fall apart. These girls are having a hard enough time.

She purses her lips. "How are you holding up?"

"Not great. How about you?"

"Awful, but I'm not as bad off as Blake." Her lip trembles, and I have to look away. "She's locked herself inside her room."

"Oh, no. Poor girl."

"Yeah—she found this letter from Mom to all of us when she went through her jewelry box to find some earrings for me. She hasn't spoken a word since then, other than to tell us to go away." She hands me a sheet of paper with Julia Caroline's beautiful handwriting scrawled from top to bottom.

Dear family,

If you're reading this, it means I'm already gone from this life. We've had so many wonderful times together, and I've been so proud to be your mom (Susan), grandmother (Blake, Elaina, and Brittany), and best friend (Nancy).

I didn't know I was dying until the pathology report came back as stage four breast cancer, on the morning when I left the hospital. I'm sorry I didn't tell you, but the doctors said it was too late for chemo or radiation to help. I didn't want to feel weaker than I already was in my last days. I hope you can understand and respect this decision.

Thank you for all your love. Lay me to rest, but I don't want you to spend a long time worrying about me ... there's no need. You know where I'll be. If you miss me, just look up. I'll be the one watching over y'all and cheering you on from Heaven.

XOXO,
Granny Mason

MY EYES MIST OVER. "She was the best, and I can't imagine what life is going to be like now. But she would definitely want all of you to live your lives to the fullest. I'm going to try talking to Blake."

Susan purses her lips. "I hope she'll come out for a while. This is the worst day of all our lives, but it isn't good for her to be alone in there."

I go upstairs and knock on her bedroom door. "Blake, let me in, hon."

No answer. I blow my bangs out of my eyes and knock again. She's hurting, but I need to know she is okay. "Hon, you'd better answer me, or I'll take this darn door off its hinges. It might take me all day, but you know I'll do it. Just tell me you're alright, and I'll leave you alone."

The door pops open. *Thank goodness!* I reach out for Blake, but she goes back to bed and covers her head with a quilt.

"I don't want to talk right now, but you saw me. I'm all in one piece. Can you tell everyone I'm okay and to give me a break? I just need to sleep. I was up all night. I thought I heard Granny Mason talking to me every time I drifted off. Mom doesn't like us mentioning woo-woo things or ghosts, so I couldn't tell her."

Oh, goodness. Julia Caroline must have been talking to Blake. Why did she scare the girl like that if she didn't want her to know about the family gift of clairvoyance?

Before I leave Blake's room, I tell her to call me when she is up to it. This is so hard, but there's no use in forcing her to talk if she isn't ready. Instead, I return to the living room, where Susan and the other girls have fallen asleep on the sofa. If Julia Caroline were here, her heart would have melted at the sight.

With Dan's sendoff being tonight, I have a mountain of preparations to get ready. Since everyone else is asleep, I decide to head home and start preparing for my date with the devil himself. I leave them a note, saying I'm going home to rest, even though nothing could be further from the truth.

Most of all, I need to find a way to draw him out of hiding and trick him into hanging out in my backyard for a spell ... *pun intended.*

This isn't a one-person job. I text Clint to ask for his help, and my boy agrees. I'm so grateful for him, but I also need someone with the ability to communicate with the dead. Now that Julia Caroline is gone, I don't know anyone else who can … except for Tom. We've had the oddest dates—if you can call them that—so why not ask?

I dial his number, and when he answers, I tell him about Julia Caroline's passing. He sighs loudly. "I'm so sorry. This definitely isn't the outcome we expected. When I shared the pathology report with her yesterday, she was alone. I asked her if she wanted me to call you or Susan to be with her, but she insisted she didn't. Did she talk to you?"

I cough and do my best to push through the conversation. "No. I didn't know until she was already gone."

"Oh, no! Why do you think she didn't tell you?"

"She left a letter saying she didn't want her family to try to convince her to go through any treatments." My voice trembles, and I pause. "Do you think they might have helped?"

"This isn't going to be easy to hear, but after reading her pathology report, I don't. This type of cancer can be so aggressive, and we found it much too late. That being said, I didn't expect her to go overnight. I would have figured she'd have at least a few months left." He pauses. "Nan, I know how hard it is to lose a friend, but I also hate seeing good people suffering and going through multiple rounds of chemo and surgeries only to die, anyway. I wouldn't wish that on my worst enemy."

Tears spill down my cheeks, and I sit silently for a moment before answering. *He's right. I didn't want Julia Caroline to suffer through all those treatments, but I'm still ticked off that she failed to share the lab results with me yesterday morning.*

I push back tears. "Thank you for your honest opinion. It helps me feel more at peace after hearing everything you shared."

"Of course. I'm here anytime you want to talk. Speaking of which, no pressure, but if you'd like me to bring you lunch or coffee, just call."

"Actually, I need a favor." I proceed to tell him what I have in mind for luring in Dan this evening. He agrees to help, and I thank him. It's good to know I won't be alone in this; come to think of it, we could probably use some more helpers.

As dead set as I was about not telling Mario's family about Dan's haunting, they might enjoy helping me kick his ghostly rear end to the curb.

I grab the letter and set out to begin the ending of Dan Sutton.

CHAPTER 28

*I*nstead of walking home, I head straight to Connie's place. A strange car is parked in the driveway. Now might not be the best time to drop by for a surprise visit, especially since I want to talk about sending spirits to the Other Side.

Lauren opens the front door. "Hey! C'mon in here. Mario's granny, Barbara, is here visiting."

"Are you sure I'm not intruding?"

"Not at all. She actually had some questions about Mario for you."

Oh, yeah! I'd forgotten she is a seer. Barbara's visit couldn't have been timed any better. We're gonna need all the help we can get, especially from someone who can communicate with the dead. Between her and Tom, I should be in good shape.

When I step inside, Connie introduces us, and I immediately notice the striking family resemblance.

Barbara smiles. "I know I look a lot older than the last time you saw me. It's probably been thirty years, give or take." She and her family lived on the island for a short time back in the late 80s and moved away. Connie and her husband moved back when Clint and Mario were in elementary school.

"I reckon I do, too, hon. But my grandson, Clint, loved Mario like a brother." I sit down on the sofa next to Lauren and fold my hands in my lap.

"Oh, believe me, I know all about those two. Mario couldn't wait to come back home and work with Clint. I was so glad to hear he had a readymade best friend and partner here. I can't believe someone shot him. He was such a good guy and an incredible police officer. I miss my guy." She wipes a tear from her cheek.

"I'm so sorry. I hope this isn't too much to ask, but Connie mentioned you can communicate with and see spirits. I could use your help and Lauren's tonight if you're both up for it."

Both women nod, and Lauren slaps her knee. "I'm ready to take Dan on. He never believed in me when we were dating, but he didn't want anyone else to have me either. Just tell us what to do."

As I explain my plans, Connie's eyes widen. "I'll stay with Georgie, so they can do whatever you need, but how did you figure all this out?"

"Unfortunately, Dan has paid me numerous unwelcome visits, mostly at the hospital."

Connie gulps. "That's horrific. God bless you for helping Mario. Speaking of the hospital, is Julia Caroline still there?"

I start to answer, but my lungs tighten, and my head begins spinning. Everything goes still and fuzzy before it fades to total darkness. I can't hear anything either. *Did I die? That would be the best punchline for this whole dadblamed joke of a week!*

Bits and pieces of conversation creep in through the nothingness, but the words don't make sense.

What seems like hours later, I wake up lying down on Connie's sofa with Clint shining a flashlight in my eyes. *What in the heck is going on? If I didn't have a stroke, I probably will now, thanks to this dang search and rescue floodlight; I mean flashlight.*

I grab his hand. "Just what in tarnation do you think you're doing? Trying to give me a seizure?"

Clint ignores my sass like usual. "Lauren called me to come over when you passed out. What did it feel like when you fell?"

I describe the moments leading up to my fit or whatever you'd call it.

Clint nods. "I think you had a panic attack. Since you didn't hit your head, I won't make you go to the hospital. I know how much you hate it, especially now, after everything that happened to Julia Caroline." He stops. "I can't believe she's gone."

Connie bites her lip. "Oh, my Lord. That's why you blacked out when I asked about her. Nan—I'm really sorry."

"It's okay. You didn't know." I wrap my arm around her. "We'll just have to support each other."

Connie laces her arm through mine and pats my back. "You got it!" I feel the slightest tinge of a smile tugging at the corners of my mouth. *Thank God for friends.*

"I'm so grateful for y'all. I need to go scrounge up a few things at my house and get mentally prepared. See you tonight."

Clint follows me out of the house. "Jump into my Jeep. I'm sticking to you like glue today, just to make sure you're okay. If I so much as see a bruise pop up on your noggin, I'm taking you to the emergency room. Any other day, I would have made you go on the spot."

I wrinkle my nose. "Who's the parent now?"

He points his finger at himself. "Me. Now do what I say."

"Well, okie dokie, then. What are we doing, sir?"

"First, I'm making you eat somethin'. I know you hardly eat anything anymore. Don't argue with me. I'll help you get ready for tonight as soon as we get some grub in you."

God bless him. Most twenty-somethings are too busy to care if their grandmothers have eaten that day, let alone within a given week. But not Clint; he's a good 'un.

When he parks in Acme's parking lot, we get out and walk

into the restaurant. My shoulders drop when we sit down and order our food. With everything we've been through, it is good to stop, clear our minds and feed our bellies. Even though I know tonight is going to be hectic, I can afford a half-hour break.

While we eat, Clint and I brainstorm our game plan. I scribble a few notes on a napkin and draw out a map of where we need everyone stationed.

He winces. "Do you think we can pull this whole crazy thing off and get rid of Dan?"

"You're darn tootin' … I sure do. He'll regret the day he set foot on Isle of Palms. We take care of our own here. And Mario was one of our finest."

Clint squeezes my hand, warming my heart. "Thanks for helping me get justice for my friend."

"Anytime … always." I'd go to the ends of the earth for any of my family.

After we pay our check, Clint and I get into the Jeep and head over to my house. I should have most of the supplies we need inside my potting shed. We walk back there, and a silvery haze appears. *Oh, gosh ... this can't be Dan, not yet.* I check my watch—it's only 4:30, not even close to midnight.

As the specter's outline solidifies, I can tell it's Mario. *Thank the Lord!* We should give him a rundown of everything we're planning, so he can help.

Mario waves and slaps his forehead. "I totally forgot Clint can't see me. I miss my pal."

I call Clint over and tell him what Mario said, and his eyes light up.

"Hey, buddy! I'm glad you're here. Your family is helping us send Dan off over yonder tonight. You should come over, too." Clint continues describing our plans to Mario, and I relay his responses back to Clint. *If the boys can get along this well without a direct line of communication, maybe I need to give Julia Caroline more of a chance. It's not like she asked to be sick or die.*

Mario says he will try to join us, but he can feel Dan's presence returning. "I'd better get back for now, but I'll try to help later. I'll see what I can do."

After his apparition fades, we return to our project, and I find five cobalt blue bottles inside the potting shed. Even though the bottling incantation only calls for one bottle, there's safety in numbers. If one of the bottles doesn't catch Dan, hopefully, one of the other four will be up to the task. I pull the corks from the bottles and set them aside before tying the bottles onto a strand of thin yet strong nautical rope. Clint reinforces each knot and helps me string the garland across a low-hanging branch on the grand oak tree in my backyard.

Tom leans over the garden gate to announce his arrival, and we motion for him to come in as we stand back and admire our work.

Clint gives me a thumbs up. "That looks really cool."

"It doesn't have as many bottles as the real deal, but it's all I had in the shed. It should still do the trick because, according to the notecard, we only need one bottle."

Tom nods. "I've always wanted a bottle tree. They're really stunning. I never considered their magical qualities. Now I really want one."

I gather the corks and place them on the windowsill for safe-keeping. I check the time on my cell phone—we've got about an hour and a half before everyone else will start showing up ... as long as everything goes according to plan.

That's plenty of time for a mug full of coffee and a slice of pecan pie with ice cream. We retreat to the kitchen for dessert and to psych ourselves up for what promises to be yet another weird night.

CHAPTER 29

*A*fter dessert, the three of us gather up the last couple of things we need and wait for a sign from Lauren and Barbara that they're nearby. I fidget with my hands to avoid picking at my fingernails and cuticles. It's a nasty nervous habit that I'm determined to break.

A woman screaming in the distance fills my house. *Was that Lauren or Barbara? It must have been.*

I place the pearls around my neck and grab the notecard before running outside. I can feel my heart beating in my throat. *Don't have a coronary, Nancy!* At least we have a doctor in the house tonight!

We gather around the oak tree, where the blue bottles reflect the moonlight.

Barbara and Lauren arrive, panting. When Barbara catches her breath and says, "Dan is almost here. It's a long story, but Lauren lured him out of hiding. I've held my rosary all night, just in case he got out of control."

My pulse races. *I hope this is the last time I ever have to think about Dan. God help us!* I clasp my hands together.

"Okay, y'all—it's almost time! We only get one shot with these pearls, so let's stay focused. Barbara, get your rosary ready, and Tom, open your Bible to Revelation. If things go sideways, read any scripture, but I have a specific one in mind for finishing out the spell."

Everyone forms a circle around the tree just as the veil of silver appears, like the morning fog sweeping over the marsh.

When Dan takes shape, stares at Lauren, and starts walking toward her. *Does he really think she wants to be with a dead man? Of course he does. What a moron.* Strangling him would feel great, but it wouldn't be helpful, seeing how he's a ghost and all. Sending him away for good will be even better.

I hold out my trembling hand and focus on reading the incantation.

"Leave the earth for a short while; gravitate in this object. This is not your final destination."

Dan becomes ever so slightly more translucent as he vies for Lauren's attention. I resist the urge to roll my eyes and mock him. Instead, I follow the notecard instructions and continue repeating the incantation.

A shimmering trail flows from Dan into one of the blue bottles, filling it a little at a time. *It's working!*

After six repetitions, a shadow of Dan's outline still remains. *Why isn't he budging?* I remember the notecard's directions say the incantation may need to be read multiple times. *Wait! There's power in numbers. I may not have Julia Caroline's help this time, but my other friends are here. Duh—I don't have to do this alone.* I ask everyone to join me in reciting the spell.

Before we start, Dan's coloring brightens ever so slightly, and the filling bottle empties completely and shatters. *Thank goodness we have four more!*

I hold my steadied palm out toward Dan. "You're not off the hook, buddy! Not on our watch!" I point to Tom, and he reads a passage from the Book of James.

"Submit yourselves, then, to God. Resist the devil, and he will flee from you."

Dan scowls as his right arm fades into nothingness. We huddle closer together and double down on reading the incantation. His apparition fades a little more each time we say the phrase, reminding me of a static-filled TV screen. Finally, after eight more reps, he appears to have disappeared. *What took so long?*

I move closer to the blue bottles. A silvery essence swirls inside one, almost like a fast-moving lava lamp.

Hallelujah! Now, the notecard instructions say to recite a Bible verse, but which one makes the most sense? With the pearls in my hand, the scripture that comes to mind is from Revelation. I pull up the verse on my phone and ask everyone to read it with me.

"And the twelve gates were twelve pearls, each of the gates made of a single pearl, and the street of the city was pure gold, like transparent glass."

Reading the scripture, I finally understand what the pearls on Julia Caroline's necklace represent—hope, faith, and protection for the person wearing them. The very love that her family poured into each pearl brings the magic to life. Despite all of Dan's transgressions toward our family and friends, I could never deny hope for someone's salvation. We have all fallen short at some point in our lives.

A sparkling glow forms around the bottle, and the silvery essence seems to be at rest inside.

Moving closer to the bottle, I cork the opening tightly and bid Dan farewell. "Your time of tormenting others here on earth is through. In your human life, you took so much from Mario's family, but it isn't my place to judge you. God has that covered. As a Christian, I know everyone deserves God's grace. I pray you find peace."

Lauren tilts her head. "What happens to him now? Can he get out of the bottle, or is he in there for good?"

I shake my head. "No. His soul will be carried to the Other Side overnight."

Lauren's eyes widen, and she kneels near the tree and looks up at the bottle. This poor woman has lost so much because of Dan. I pray she can find happiness and hope for her and Georgie's future.

Barbara lets out a low cry. "I can't believe that man killed Mario. I wish I could have said goodbye to my precious grandson."

I blink. "You haven't seen him at Connie's place?"

"No. I just got into town right before you stopped by to ask for our help."

I call out for Mario. Now that Dan is out of the picture, he should be free to move as he wishes. I hope he can hear me.

A silvery mist forms, and Mario's face solidifies. *Praise the Lord!*

Barbara falls to her knees, and tears spill down her cheeks. "My boy. I'm so happy to see you. And I'm so proud of who you grew up to be."

Lauren hangs her head, and Clint pats her back. "It isn't fair. I wish I could see him, but I'm glad Georgie and his granny have." She closes her eyes. "No one should have to lose someone they love so suddenly."

I shake my pointer finger at her. "There's a whole lotta truth there." When I look back over toward the house, I see Julia Caroline.

She frowns. "Hang on, Nan. You know I didn't choose this."

Barbara's forehead wrinkles. "Tell me when you passed again."

Julia Caroline purses her lips. "Yesterday." How can she say it so matter-of-factly when she knows how badly I'm hurting?

Barbara sighs. "Oh, boy. I see. Hey, Lauren and Mario—we need to let these people deal with their own grief. C'mon. Let's go home."

Lauren frowns. "What am I missing?"

I wince. "It's Julia Caroline." I place my hand on Lauren's arm. "Hon, I'll stop by and chat with y'all soon. I really need to talk to her."

Lauren opens her mouth as if she wants to say something, but closes it and nods. She and Barbara say their goodbyes, and I sit down on the concrete bench in my garden.

Clint sits down next to me. "Is Julia Caroline here?"

Tom waves at her. "She sure is, and I'm taking this as my cue to leave, too. I know y'all have a lot to discuss. I'll call you tomorrow, Nan." He kisses my cheek and leaves the garden.

Julia looks upward. "Nan, you know darn well that we don't get to pick how and when we go. Why are you able to forgive Dan, a murderer, but not me? I didn't kill anyone. Don't I deserve the same grace?"

I lock eyes with her and growl. "You should have shared the pathology results. I would have come to the hospital to be there with you."

"I told you already … no treatments could have helped save my life. It wouldn't have done any good."

I throw my hands up in the air, and I can feel the vein in my forehead pulsating. "Maybe not, but you didn't even give me the chance to process the news with you. Didn't I deserve the opportunity to be there for you? At least it would have been less of a shock when died so suddenly. Instead, I thought you would make a full recovery. I get that these things can change on the turn of a dime, but you have to understand that I'm hurtin' really bad. Wouldn't you be upset if our roles were reversed?"

Julia Caroline's shoulders drop, and she places her hand over her mouth. "I didn't think of it that way. I would be in absolute agony. I should have told you, but I didn't know how. It's just not a conversation I ever thought we'd have. I'm so sorry. I love you, and I'm not planning to cross over until I absolutely have to. I don't want to miss a thing."

Tears stream down my face, and I try to stop sobbing, but I can't.

Clint squeezes my hand. "I don't know what Julia Caroline is saying, but I'm glad you're able to talk to her. I wish Mario would appear to me, so we can have another conversation before he's gone."

I straighten a little and wipe my eyes. "I'm so sorry, son. I've made this night all about me instead of focusing on helping your friend and his family. If you want to go with me to Connie's tomorrow, I'll help you talk to Mario. You're a good friend."

He nods. "I want to do everything I can for his family and for you, too. Gram—I'm gonna stay the night in my old room tonight. Come get me if you need anything. I love you."

"I love you too, sweetheart."

As he walks inside the house, I thank God for sending me this complete angel of a grandson. In a time when so many young people want nothing to do with their families, I couldn't be more blessed. Which reminds me, what about Susan and her girls? Where did Julia Caroline go?

"Hey, are you still here?"

She appears out of the shadow of the oak tree and furrows her brow. "It depends … are you done beating me up?"

"It depends … are you going to let me know if you decide to move to the Other Side for good?"

She shrugs. "As long as it's within my control. I know a lot about sending spirits to their Final Destination, but I don't know much about when the transition happens randomly or how to choose to stay here. My husband is waiting for me over there, but I'm hoping he can find a way to break away to see me here … even though he never did before. Maybe he can't."

"Okay, okay. I don't want to argue anymore." I draw a deep breath, and Julia Caroline glares at me as I turn to walk into my house. *Let her squirm for a bit. She has put me in a bad spot, and I'm not done being hurt. Childish or not, I need to chew on this until all the flavor runs out. It would be nice if that happens tomorrow, but my heart is so tender. Who knows when or if it will? I've earned my right to be emotional.*

I head upstairs to my bedroom without pausing, in case she is following me, and close my door. Collapsing onto my bed, I sob for hours before eventually crying myself to sleep.

CHAPTER 30

*I*n the morning, I get up and brace myself for another hard day with Susan and the girls. *How dare Julia Caroline die first! Who gave her permission?*

Why didn't she prepare all of us better for this situation? All it would have taken is her saying, "Hey. So, the doctor told me I could go any day now." Would we have been upset? Absolutely, we would have been distraught beyond belief. But at least I wouldn't be carrying around this horrible feeling that my best friend deceived me.

As I pad my way down the steps, I hear someone moving around in the kitchen. I freeze in place. *Did something go wrong with the bottling incantation? Is Dan waiting to pick a fight with me? I don't want to deal with him. And he doesn't want to mess with me either. Today ain't the day, mister!*

When I walk downstairs, Clint is standing over the stove, flipping pancakes. *Oh, goodness, I totally forgot ... he stayed over last night. I'm glad I didn't come charging into the room with my cross pendant and Bible, ready to pounce.*

I try to collect myself, so I don't look too bonkers. "Morning, hon. How did you sleep?"

"Eh ... not great. I'm sure you didn't rest either. But before you say too much else, you should know Blake is here."

My eyes widen. "What did she say? Where is she?"

Clint motions for me to lower my voice and nods toward the powder room between the living room and kitchen. "She's in the bathroom. I can tell she's been crying pretty freaking hard. She wants to talk to both of us at the same time. I'd planned to come get you after I finished cooking these flapjacks, which sounded tasty, but now I'm not so sure."

He wrinkles his nose and groans as he piles an overflowing stack of fluffy pancakes onto a plate.

Ugh, is right ... my stomach churns and gurgles. Those pancakes would hit me like a ton of bricks if I tried to eat even a couple of those hefty suckers. *Dang it.* I haven't been eating properly lately, and I doubt today will be any better. I've always had a healthy appetite, so this is uncharted territory for me.

The powder room door creaks open, and the little bit of food inside my stomach threatens to come up. I'm not ready for this conversation! Blake walks toward us with her head hanging down. *Oh, my heart! This is going to be tough.*

I'm only holding together for this poor child's sake. "Tell me what's on your mind, hon."

She sits down at the kitchen table and lays her head down, sobbing.

I hold her, and we both cry. There are no words to make it better. We've lost our anchor in the sea of life. Blake always turned to Julia Caroline with any problem she couldn't solve on her own. Some of their kinfolk criticized Susan and Jeremy, saying they left the real parenting up to her grandmother. But that wasn't it at all.

They're wonderful parents; it's just that Blake and her granny took up with each other in an almost supernatural way ... like how people talk about the spiritual connection between twins. They were two peas in a pod. It makes complete sense that she is taking it so hard ... not that the rest of us aren't.

When she calms, she wipes her cheeks. "I needed to get out of there. We're all devastated, but I know you get what I'm feeling the most. Life will never be the same. I just can't believe she is gone."

"Me either," I whisper. *I hope Julia Caroline can hear what we're saying. She needs to know how deeply her death is cutting us.*

Blake rubs her eyes. "Is it okay if I hang out here for a while? I just need a break. There are too many memories at Granny Mason's house, and it's weird; I can't quite explain it, but I feel like she's still there with me."

I want to scream, "It's because she is!" But I don't, out of respect for Julia Caroline's wishes.

"Of course, hon. You know you're always welcome here. I've gotta run out to the garden for a few minutes. Help yourself to some of these pancakes Clint made and watch TV. I'll be back shortly."

I slip on my shoes and go outside. The blue bottles strung from the oak tree glisten in the sun and move gently in the breeze. I clench my jaw as I examine the corked bottle—it's completely empty! *Hallelujah!* I hope and pray that means Dan has moved on to the Other Side, never to be seen on earth again. The world will undoubtedly be a better place for it.

Whether or not I've forgiven him, no one needs to endure the terror he delivered to Mario's family.

As frustrating and dangerous as this gift of communicating with the dead can be at times, there are some benefits. Without it, I wouldn't be able to protect my loved ones from evil spirits or help them say goodbye to people they care about. Tears sting my eyes when I consider what life would be like right now if I couldn't talk to Julia Caroline. I'd be beyond inconsolable. I'm hurting like I took a bite out of a hornet nest, but at least I've said my piece. So few people have that luxury. I've gotta let go of my fury.

When I open the kitchen door, I can hear Blake and Clint talking over the television in the living room. These young people deserve the best of everything, and I know they'd find it in each other again if they gave it a chance. *Hmm. Maybe I should leave them alone for a bit longer.* I know both of them are at a vulnerable point in their lives. They could help each other process the pain.

I return to the garden and sit down on the bench again. *What a wild and confusing spiral of events this week!*

After we lay Julia Caroline's body to rest, I'm not lifting a finger for at least a month. Nope. My butt is going to be planted on a comfy beach chair until at least Labor Day. If anyone wants to talk to me, they're more than welcome to pull up a seat next to mine, unless I'm reading. Then, they'd better button their lips and wait until I'm good and ready for a conversation. I have quite a backlog of books to read.

I lie down on the bench. Despite it being concrete, I can usually get pretty comfortable lying on it.

Julia Caroline appears in an iridescent mist beside the sweeping grand oak and holds out her hand. "Hang on. Before you get fired up again, I have something to say. Deal?"

I want to slap her face, but I doubt she'd feel it. It ain't worth hurting my stirring hand. So, I just nod. "I suppose. You should know Blake is in there with Clint. They were talking, so I came out here to give them some space."

She raises her eyebrows. "Do you think there might still be even a small spark between them?" I shrug. "The way they reacted to seeing each other at the hospital tells me it's a possibility. No one gets that upset by bumping into someone they don't care about. But only time will tell. Susan told me Blake is dating some guy, though. I'm trying not to get my hopes up yet."

Julia Caroline scowls. "Oh, you mean that loser, Parker? Let me tell ya, that man isn't worthy of our amazing girl. Susan and I have known it from the get-go. And to beat everything, he's a blasted Sutton."

"You're kidding! He's one of *those* Suttons? As in, he's kin to

Dan and the nasty couple who let all their employees die in the hotel fire on Sweetgrass Island in the 80s?"

"Yep. He's one of Reginald and DeeDee's boys. Dan was his cousin, but he grew up in California. I don't know the whole story about why his parents lived on the West Coast, but the Suttons were the absolute worst family from our neck of the woods. Reginald and DeeDee moved to Knoxville to start over shortly after the fire. From what I've heard, they've built quite the underhanded law firm, creating shady deals with the lowest scum in the Southeast. No surprises there, considering how slimy and corrupt they've always been. I've tried telling Blake that Parker isn't worth her time, but she won't hear a word about it. Maybe she'll listen to you."

"Geez, Louise! Out of all the people she could have dated ... I'll try talking to her about Parker when the timing is right, but this ain't it. You need to let the poor girl grieve the death of her granny. She is beyond devastated; rightfully so."

Julia Caroline winces. "I don't want her or any of y'all to hurt. Speaking of which, how are you feeling? Have you found it in your heart to forgive me yet?"

My heart sinks. I can't very well hold a grudge against a ghost, especially my best friend's spirit. It seems like she is going to stick around for as long as she can. When it comes down to it, I suppose our lives don't have to be all that different. I'll have to find a way to prevent looking like I belong on a nut farm while talking to her in public.

"I forgive you, but I'm still hurtin' somethin' fierce. It's just because I love you so dadburn much. I'm trying to let go of the anger. I really am—I promise. It's all just so very fresh. Give me some time for it not to sting quite as bad."

She embraces me, and I jump at the tingling sensation that runs through my body. I rarely touch spirits, so I forget how similar it can feel to touching a living person—the only thing missing is the warmth of blood flowing through their veins. Usually, when I'm around ghosts, I'm too busy figuring out how to send them to the Other Side … either because they're causing chaos, or they've asked for help reaching their final resting place. Plus, I don't make it a habit to touch too many people, dead or alive. To be fair, I'm not crazy about helping most people or spirits. They're not worth the trouble.

But there's only one Julia Caroline Mason.

She may no longer be of this crazy world, but she is still part of mine. Even though things are different now, her presence and friendship matter most.

CHAPTER 31

*L*ater that afternoon, Susan and her girls joined me for a walk along the beach. We don't talk much as we walk, but being together warms my soul.

Waves lap along the shoreline, splashing our bare feet. Pouring salt on a wound might hurt, but here on the island, we know saltwater heals even the deepest cuts. It's a necessary part of our healing process.

When we reach the pier, I stand still and close my eyes. A warm breeze grazes my shoulders. I reckon this is as close as I can get to experiencing Heaven while I'm still on earth.

There is no pain in Heaven. Here, letting go of the hurt we're experiencing will take a while, but crying an endless ocean of tears isn't going to bring Julia Caroline back. I feel someone wrap their arm around my shoulder, and I open my eyes to see Blake standing close to me.

I pat her hand. "Are you okay, hon?"

"As good as I can be. I feel better by the water. Being in Granny Mason's house is hard because I expect to see her walk into the room at any minute. Down here on the beach, I feel like she is already with me. It hurts less. Does that make sense?"

Out of the corner of my eye, I notice a silvery bubble materialize, and Julia Caroline appears.

What impeccable timing! I nod. "She loved this beach more than any other place in the world. It only makes sense that you feel her presence here. And I'm glad you have that connection with her."

"Me too. And being with you helps. I love you."

A tear spills down my cheek, and I smile as I wipe it away. "I'm so happy to be part of your family, hon. I love you, too. As long as we have each other to get through losing your granny, we'll find a way to keep going."

Blake kisses my cheek and runs ahead to catch up with her mom and sisters, who appear to be scanning the shoreline for shells. I hang back to talk to Julia Caroline. When the other ladies grow smaller in the distance, I turn to my best friend's spirit.

"Where do we go from here? What am I supposed to do now?"

Julia Caroline holds my hand. "You're already doing it. Thank you for loving my girls as much as I do. It gives me peace knowing they have someone on this side of Heaven."

"But you're not going for good yet, right?"

"Nope, but there is someone who has been patiently waiting for me. I need to go see him." She gestures toward the sky, where James stands, radiating a silver iridescent beam. How can I deny them the opportunity to be together? For a decade, they have been apart, and I now understand the pain of losing a soulmate. While our relationship was sisterly, not romantic, losing Julia Caroline as my earthly companion has shredded my heart into a billion jagged pieces.

"I get it, but don't forget us here. We love you so much."

Julia Caroline smiles broadly. "I couldn't ever forget any of you. I'll be seeing you soon."

She drifts upward toward James, and he holds out his hand. As my best friend grasps her one true love's hand, a glow encapsulates them. She turns back toward me and blows me a kiss right before they vanish into a silvery mist.

Tears sting my eyes. If anyone deserves a happily ever after, it's Julia Caroline. I'll find mine with our lovely families. Who knows? Maybe Tom will stick around, too.

BOOKS BY STEPHANIE EDWARDS

- **Lowcountry Charm:** A Palm Court Suspense, Book 1 (prequel to the Isle of Palms Suspense series)
- **Charleston Grit:** A Palm Court Suspense, Book 2 (prequel to the Isle of Palms Suspense series)
- **The Haunting on Palm Court:** An Isle of Palms Suspense, Book 1
- **Return to Palm Court:** An Isle of Palms Suspense, Book 2
- **Christmas on Palm Court:** An Isle of Palms Suspense, Book 3
- **The Word Dancer:** An Appalachian Tale (standalone)

Visit stephedwardswrites.com for more details.

www.ingramcontent.com/pod-product-compliance
Lightning Source LLC
Chambersburg PA
CBHW071744150726
47998CB00005B/1796